A SINGLE DEGREE OF FREEDOM

An Exploration of Faith, Love and Loss in a Medical Practice

Bernard Mc Cann MD

Printed in Victoria, BC, Canada.

ISBN: 978-1-4269-3135-2 (sc)

ISBN: 978-1-4269-3136-9 (e-book)

Library of Congress Control Number: 2010905174

Our mission is to efficiently provide the world's finest, most comprehensive book publishing service, enabling every author to experience success. To find out how to publish your book, your way, and have it available worldwide, visit us online at www.trafford.com

Trafford rev. 4/7/2010

 www.trafford.com

North America & international
toll-free: 1 888 232 4444 (USA & Canada)
phone: 250 383 6864 ✦ fax: 812 355 4082

Authors Note

This is a work of fiction. Any resemblance to any person, place or institution is unintended. Nevertheless, it is true that all fiction has some basis in reality. This story could have been told as a bare clinical history in which the patient and the physician are reduced to abstractions. No human encounter leaves the participants unchanged, and this is especially true in medicine. For readers unfamiliar with medical terms and concepts, a glossary has been appended.

Thanks are due to Elsa Mondou M.D. for her careful reading of the manuscript and for her helpful suggestions. I am especially grateful for her friendship and support.

FORWARD

Sarah was forty-five when she died. She had been hospitalized two and one-half months. Her discharge summary (death summary) was three pages long. Her hospital chart was four volumes. The medical board hearing transcript about my actions ran over four hundred pages. None of that tells Sarah's story or mine.

My daughter was a second year medical student at the time and thus still idealistic. My lawyer needed a narrative to build a defense or in my view, an explanation. For my daughter and others with significant medical knowledge, the medical descriptions will seem simplistic. For lawyers, you can't make it too simple.

Still, with thirty-five years of medical practice on the line and I suppose, my identity as a physician and human being as well, I need to understand how I came to be in this stuffy hearing room charged with euthanasia if not outright murder. This account began after my daughter mailed an angry letter, enclosing clippings from the Boston Globe with a lurid account of the case. Although I was not named, she read between the lines and asked "Dad, Why?"

CHAPTER I

Dear Kathleen,

Your last letter indicated that the Eastern newspapers had finally printed articles about this incident. I haven't wanted to discuss this with you until you had some clinical experience. Now that your medical education is sufficiently advanced, you will be in a better position to understand what I did and why.

The Medical Board is now in executive session, to consider sanctioning me and possibly making a criminal referral because of allegations of serious ethical lapses in Sarah's care. This is the second day of the hearing. We are on the second floor in a conference room in a featureless building near the airport. The only window gives a splendid view of the same style building next door and is the mausoleum for six dead flies and one creature whose advanced state of decomposition makes precise classification impossible. There is a faint odor of tobacco smoke in the air despite the sign on the wall and state law. There are three physicians including the chairman, two attorneys, a "public" member and the board's attorney. All are political appointees and friends of the governor. One physician still has an active practice in dermatology. The oldest has been retired for years, is probably senile and sleeps through most of the session. I suspect that the last medical textbook he saw was written by

1

Galen. The chairman was appointed by the conservative Republican governor as a favor to the religious right whose support he needed to counter the Democratic advantage in the southern part of the state.

Ever since the legislature tried to cut their budget, the board has been actively soliciting complaints from the public and posting them on their website. The hearings are closed to the public and the transcripts are sealed except for portions leaked to journalists known for their tabloid style. Due process is limited- the physician can attempt to rebut charges but cannot see evidence or cross examine witnesses. There is no provision for appeal.

The first day had been consumed by the board's attorney reading into the record selected portions of the medical records and the statements of anonymous witnesses. Now it's our turn. The facts are not in dispute, I did what I did. My motivation is the issue.

The story from the Boston papers that you sent is essentially a copy of the local reporters work down to the running headline

'Mercy Killing- Doctor's Assisted Suicide of His Lover'

In addition to being lurid and wrong, they didn't bother to cite the local reporter's byline. Well, no honor among thieves. Of course, they did not get the whole story that played out here over several weeks and in a sense, continues even now months later. It was not helpful that the local leader of the Hemlock Society wrote a letter to the editor in my defense, which prompted the Catholic bishop to write an Op-Ed piece in reply. The same Bishop forcibly retired Father Francis even though the old priest's confessional seal was intact. Jean, who was present at the end, is still head nurse on the neuro ward, but neither of us talks about it. There is no need. A hospital like St. James is like a small town where we spend most of our waking hours. Our personal and professional successes are known and much more so our personal and professional failures. The latter are often formally examined in medical mortality conferences and critical incident reviews. The failures that are both become part of the stories that abound here.

I will try to tell my story and, of course, part of Sarah's. Because of the allegations of ethical improprieties, I will have to explore for you my understanding of the ethical imperatives, the rules of engagement in this war on disease. I don't know who filed the allegations with the board, or what narrative was conveyed. Suffice it to say that the board wants to connect the relationship that Sarah and I briefly enjoyed to her death as cause and effect. Knowing your loyalty to your mother, I will try to be as clear as possible about that relationship. Still, even now, I'm not sure I fully understand my motivation. I can only hope for your merciful understanding.

Since the episode has been in the papers and every politician and fanatic has weighed in, the Board will do what is expedient. The only two people who understand this are she and I, and she is dead. Maybe after reading this you will think of me kindly sometime.

I guess I just wanted to tell you how it was, so you could see it was not the cold calculated act they depicted for the record. She was not the first person I have watched die and she won't be the last, but she was the hardest. The hundreds of others that I declared brain dead and stopped support, the terminal stroke patients going out on a cloud of Dilaudid and diazepam, most of those were not really there. She was there to the end to the final push of morphine and just as I pushed the drug IV she looked at me and mouthed "I love you".

I can still see the family at the foot of the bed, the sight of the mountains out the east window, the nurse watching the monitor and then the bradycardia and widening QRS complex leading to the flat line and the monitor alarm that the nurse then switched off.

During the critical incident review that followed, I remember saying through the tears, "It's a good thing this is so hard." And it was, mostly because it was done for a friend out of love and respect and because she wanted it that way.

For the last month that she was on the ward, on the respirator, she was a vital part of our lives and especially of mine. Despite her limitations, she reached out to me in a way no one ever did before. I now know that she initially suspected that she would not leave the hospital alive especially, since at the start, I had no clear diagnosis and then when I thought I knew what was wrong, the therapies brought only limited and transient success. After two months, when we moved her out of ICU and again tried and failed to wean her from the ventilator, I think she knew for certain that she would never breathe on her own, never taste food, sing, laugh out loud or experience physical love and sex., not ever again.

It sometimes happens that a patient becomes more than a diseased human being, more than another of God's children to whom we owe a duty. Some will reach into our souls, for better or worse. Tennyson wrote

"I am a part of all that I have met"

So it was with her. Going over this again is like living it twice. The feelings come flooding back, after they have been carefully put away under the professional veneer. Her death left me with a subtle sense of hollowness and unease, rather like a first faint sense of perpetual hunger or a vague sense of fear. I wish there were a better way to tell the story than a blunt recitation of the medical facts. I recall a fragment of a poem by T.S. Elliot

"As the soul leaves the body torn and bruised
As the mind deserts the body it has used
I should find some way incomparably light and deft
Some way we both could understand
Simple and faithless as a smile and shake of the hand."

OK. So I'll tell you how it happened.

CHAPTER 2

Her name was Sarah.

Sarah Smith, which is not her real last name, came to be my patient in September of 19--. I first saw her in the emergency department (ED) of St. James Regional Medical Center. I was working our usual neurology ED call rotation, Monday, Wednesday, and Friday, Saturday, Sunday and then Tuesday, and then Thursday and then off call for a week. Its twelve straight days with seven days on twenty-four hour call. It was a late Friday afternoon. I had finished an abbreviated morning office schedule and had received the call list from the three other neurologists in our call group. I was waiting for the list from the University group as calls started to come in from the outlying hospitals that are in the catchment area of our northern Great Basin region. The catchment region, for us, is basically any hospital within helicopter range. I know you think the area is mostly sagebrush, cows and coyotes, but the town has grown a lot since you went away to college and then med school. Sometimes it's a lot for two moderate size hospitals to handle. With only four of us to cover ninety percent of the hospital neurology, I build up an enormous REM sleep deficit and have nights of continuous dreams once I finally get to sleep through the night.

Most of the rural hospitals get nervous about sick patients over the weekend and will try to transfer any patient they can sell to us. I had just accepted a transfer of a patient with a small cerebral hemorrhage, when the call came from St. James ED. The ED physician, Dr. Bannister told a story about young women with a vague two-day history of progressive slurred speech, double vision and four- extremity weakness, who had been brought in by her daughter. He thought she was having a stroke and wanted an evaluation for use of a thrombolytic drug.

Since you left, St. James has become not only the regional trauma center but now is also a regional stroke center with standing protocols for acute stroke treatment including the use of thrombolytic drugs. Bannister's voice had some urgency in it, rather than the slow, almost southern drawl I had come to expect. Bannister had labs and a head CT done before I reached the ED and it didn't take more than a minute or two to review the scans and labs. Everything looked normal; there was no sign of infection, diabetes or renal failure. He had not done blood gases but her pulse oximetry showed a slightly reduced percent of blood oxygen which is not unusual for our high altitude area. Bannister's notes and the initial triage nurse note were sketchy but didn't depict a woman who was clinically unstable when admitted to the ED.

The ED has two hallways with single rooms on each side and the hallways are separated by a central, two-sided nursing station crammed with physicians, nurses and technicians all trying to use limited numbers of computer screens. Room 12 was at the end of one of the long hallways, and when I slid open the door, things were not as advertised. The first thing I saw, in the dim light, was her fear and the shallow, panting breathing, like an overheated dog. When I went to the side of the gurney to get a better look at her face, she grabbed my hand and barely whispered "Help me ". Her eyes were half closed but the right eyelid was lower. Her face barely moved, and her grip on my hand slowly weakened. I didn't take a medical genius to know that this woman was about to die and knew it. The nurse has quietly entered the room after me and I sensed her presence behind me. I said "She's crashing, respiratory failure. Call a code-now!" She slid back the door and pivoted quickly and left, returning with an Ambu bag and mask. She clamped the mask to Sarah's face and started to ventilate the patient as the overhead speaker blared, "Code Blue ED room 12".

Bannister rushed in pushing the crash cart followed by a small mob of nurses, technicians and aides. He took one look at her and said, "She wasn't like this fifteen minutes ago." He immediately broke the seals on the crash cart, as another nurse probed Sarah's right arm for a better IV line. From the cart, Bannister pulled out vials of midazolam, succinylcholine, and a bottle of lidocaine spray. From a lower drawer, he pulled a straight blade laryngoscope, and an endotracheal tube.

He ordered the nurse "Draw up 2 mg of midazolam, 30 mg of succinylcholine, give the midazolam first,then the succcinycholine." She gave the midazolam as an IV push, then after 30 seconds slowly pushed the succinylcholine. Sarah's eyes slowly closed and her hand went limp. I had expected some muscle twitching before the paralysis, but none occurred.

"Dr. Bannister, did you give the full 30 mg?"I asked

"I must have, she's totally flaccid" he replied.

He pulled her lower jaw down, sprayed lidocaine into the back of her throat, grasped the straight blade laryngoscope in his left hand and the ET tube in his right, slid the scope onto the back of her tongue, lifted up and out and slid the ET tube between her vocal cord and into her trachea. He checked the depth by the marks on the tube, listened to both lungs while the nurse squeezed the Ambu bag. Satisfied that both lungs were being ventilated, he taped the tube in place, inflated the cuff and hooked up the volume- cycled ventilator, dialed in the settings and ordered a chest X-ray to check the tube placement

We had bought some time for us to think and for her to live.

7

Now Bannister and I needed to talk this through and decide what to do next. Both of us stepped out of the room and slid the door closed. We both stepped out of the way as the X-ray tech pushed the portable X-ray machine up to the room.

"What the hell is going on with her?" he asked. "I think this a brainstem stroke and if we don't use the thrombolytic, we will lose her." I wanted to ask why the staff let her go so far. I thought for a second and said, " I'm not sure this a stroke, and if it is, it began over three hours ago and if we are too late with the thrombolytic, she will bleed into her brainstem and we will lose her for sure. Since neither of us knows precisely when this started, or what it is, let's get an MRI done, at least with a diffusion scan. If it's negative, then we can forget about stroke."

He agreed. "I'll call radiology and have them bump the next patient "

A great idea but a logistic problem. For reasons known only to accountants and lawyers, at St. James, the MRI units are not in the hospital, but in an adjoining office building. Also, because of the high strength magnetic field, the volume cycled respirator could not be used as it has metal parts. So she had to be loaded onto a non-magnetic gurney, and rolled 660 feet to the MRI unit while being ventilated by a nurse using an Ambu bag, together with the IV poles, pumps and portable cardiac monitor.

How do I know its 660 feet? I must have walked it a thousand times in my 15 years here, and counted my steps just to clear my mind.

I tagged along, wanting to see the images and too impatient to wait for the radiologist to call with his decision. The MRI tech was an older man, perhaps 5 to 10 years my junior, with a weathered face and a ponytail and an "I don't give a shit attitude." I suspected and later knew that we shared a time and a history- the stench of rotting vegetation, monsoon rains and blue water turning to brown.

Most of my neurology training had taken place before computerized imaging had appeared. I had watched CT and MRI technology develop and knew it abolished dangerous, painful and uncertain neurodiagnostic procedures like pneumoencephalograms. Nevertheless, in my secret soul I felt it was cheating. A good neurologist ought to get the diagnosis with a safety pin, a reflex hammer, and a broken tongue blade. This is rubbish of course. Speed and certainty count more than ego and romantic notions. In any event, now that Sarah was paralyzed with neuromuscular blocking drug, neurologic exam was futile.

Most hospitals are noisy places, what with monitors and IV pumps beeping, the overhead paging system, and the constant ringing of phones. By contrast the MRI rooms are cool and quiet and as dark as a tomb. Sarah was rolled into the scanner, still being ventilated by the nurse. She was hooked up to pressure cycled respirator that was all plastic and driven by pressurized air. Similar respirators were abandoned from general use 20 years ago because they could not reliably ventilate lungs stiffened by disease.

The only light was a dimmed desk lamp and the glow of the monitor screens on the MRI console. The tech set the parameters into the console, starting with the diffusion weighted scan first. The buzzing sound of the magnets could be faintly heard through the thick walls. Slowly the images appeared on the screen, starting at the base of the skull and moving up and forward to the nose. They were normal. Even the blood vessels looked normal.

The nurse was a very young woman, or so she seemed to me, red headed, with a long distance runner's body. She seemed very fit and was not the least intimidated by a senior physician. Keeping one eye on the cardiac and respiratory monitor, she asked "So, what are we looking at?"

I asked, "What do you know about MRI?" , thinking at the same time that she looked a lot like your sister.

She said, "Not much was taught in nursing school except that radiation was not involved."

At last, a teachable moment.

I said, "The MRI scanner is a huge tubular superconducting magnet, bathed in liquid nitrogen. The magnetic field is stronger at one end than at the other. The physics are relatively simple. The human body is mostly water, which has 2 hydrogen atoms, whose nuclei behave as little magnets and align themselves along the lines of the magnetic field. Another magnetic field is applied perpendicular to the main field and pushes the nuclei out of alignment when turned on. When the field is off, the nuclei flip back and give off energy in the form of radio waves. The time to flip back depends on the surrounding molecules. Their location in the magnetic field determines the frequency of the energy given off, and thus a picture of the chemistry of the brain can be constructed by computers. When tissue dies, the movement of water in the tissue changes, so that a stroke can be seen on MRI within an hour rather than the 24-48 hours it takes for stroke to appear on a CT scan. Also the flowing blood can be imaged to give a picture of the major blood vessels in the brain."

She said, "It sounds simple but it takes all this equipment and computers to make it real. So, what do you think is going on with her?"

That is the paradox of medicine, a lot of time, money and people to develop the concepts and a lot more time, money and people to make it real and it is all applied to one suffering human being at a time. I had to think a moment to answer her question.

Logically, her weakness and respiratory failure were due to muscle or nerve disease, not stroke. The list of disease possibilities was not long, but working this out was going to take some time. Time we had, as long as we could support her breathing and vital functions. As the table slid out of the MRI tube, I noticed the Sarah seemed to be starting to move a little, as though the sedation and neuromuscular blocking agent was wearing off. The radiology tech and the nurse slid her onto the gurney and rolled her out of the MRI room to the control room. To get a better look at her, I stepped to the side of the gurney and she turned her head slightly toward me. I said, "Ma'am, I know you're scared, but we will get you through this. Just hang on for a while." That got me a fleeting smile. The nurse reattached her endotracheal tube to the Ambu bag and started the long trip back to the ED.

What to do next? The beeper had gone off three times while waiting for the MRI images, and two of the calls were from the ED. I had to go back there to write up my notes and get some orders written and talk to the pulmonary medicine specialists who would manage her ventilator and IV fluids. Sarah was only one of fifteen to twenty sick people that I would have to care for that weekend. There was neither the time nor the emotional resources to deal with each and every aspect of their care. Mostly all I can do is try to make the diagnosis and start treatment and then move on to the next patient. Sometimes all I can remember are the case details, rather than their names. I know that seems cold, but emotional involvement drains energy and clouds the mind.

Bannister had two more people for me to see, and had had the CT scans done in the scanner across the hall from the ED. The first was on the screen as I arrived. Just as in MRI, CT scan images run from skull base to the top of the skull. The first image showed all I needed to know. There was blood around the brainstem, and the second image showed a massive hemorrhage into the lower and middle brainstem. This was going to be a fatal event and I knew that there was no point in asking the neurosurgeons to intervene. A quick chart review told the story of an older Hispanic lady with an irregular heart rhythm who was taking the blood thinner coumadin. The coagulation studies showed that the blood clotting time was much more prolonged than was needed to protect her from blood clots to her brain from the heart As you have probably learned by now in pharmacology, coumadin is a tricky drug to use. It is hard to predict the proper dose because people differ in their ability to metabolize the drug and other drugs can affect its breakdown.

Going into the room, I was met by a very attractive young Hispanic woman who I assumed was a daughter or niece. She was wearing a low cut blouse and short skirt which had the look of a uniform, suggesting she was a cocktail waitress in one of the local casinos. There was no one else in the room.

The patient was already intubated and on a ventilator, and she did not seem to be initiating any breathing on her own. She had no response to pain stimulation and her pupils did not constrict to bright light. Moving her head from side to side showed me that her eyes did not move as they should. This very brief test showed that her brainstem function had been destroyed. Although she was still technically alive, her fate was sealed when the bleeding started.

I turned to the young woman and said, "This looks really bad. She has had a massive hemorrhage into the back part of her brain where all the centers that control blood pressure and breathing are located. I don't think she will make it through the night."

I had expected a question or a comment. Instead, she threw her arms around my neck and was sobbing on my shoulder. I held her gently, smelling her perfume and hoping that no one would misinterpret the scene. When she had regained some composure, I asked her, "Did she have a particular religious preference?" Despite the name, St. James is a secular institution and does not routinely record religious preference. She replied "She is Catholic, doctor"

"I'll ask the Catholic chaplain to see her as soon as possible. Are there other family members here?"

"Si, doctor"

Since she clearly spoke and understood English and had no accent, I assumed that she was probably reverting to her primary language under stress.

We stepped out in the hall and I turned to the nurse and asked her to call Fr. Francis, the elderly Catholic priest whose sole ministry was chaplain to St. James. He had given up a parish ministry to minister to the sick and dying, and his bent, white haired figure was a fixture at St. James. He would hear confession in the nursing station utility rooms and was ready to deliver the Sacrament most hours of the night. He was probably the last person many saw as the lights went out. I took her arm and we walked to the automatic double doors leading to the waiting room. As we walked, the overhead page blared, "Trauma Blue –single car roll over with passenger ejection, two minutes out" The thumping of the helicopter clearing the pad outside the ED could be faintly heard over the other noise. Often two helicopters would be in service, one on the pad and one in the park across the street. The park also was the only landing site for the large military craft occasionally used in high altitude rescues.

Entering the waiting room revealed small groups of people and singles, some huddled together, some watching TV and others staring at the doors we had just entered. She led me to a far corner where there was a group of elderly men, some kids and one or two middle aged women, all clearly Hispanic. The kids were rolling a soccer ball around while the adults talked. She spoke to one old man who seemed to be the spokesman, and in a flurry of Spanish seemed to explain who I was. I then told him what I had seen on the CT and what I thought it meant. With brief interruptions for her to translate, I gave my speech. Then there was a series of back and forth exchanges between family members, little of which I caught. After that, the old man grasped my hand and said "Muchas gracias, Doctor"

She turned to me and said "They said that she was an old woman and she did not want to be on a respirator. The want you to take her off life support after the priest sees her."
I said "Tell them I agree with their decision and offer my condolences for their loss" There was another rapid exchange in Spanish and she said "They thank you and ask when they can see her" I said "Right now would be OK. I'll talk to the nurse" She gave me another quick hug and whispered in my ear "God bless you, doctor"

In the fifteen or so years that I have practiced at St .James, I've been the bearer of bad news more often than not and I am still amazed at how people react to a message of disaster. Women will almost always hug someone, usually family, but lacking that, the evil messenger. Men will stare, shake hands but rarely hug. Most of all, they express gratitude, for the end of uncertainty, I suppose.

I left her and walked back to the nursing station and wrote the orders for what is known as comfort care – discontinue ventilator, extubate, morphine 2-4 mg IV every hour as needed for distress, two nurses may pronounce death. I sometimes wonder who we are comforting, the patient, the family or ourselves. Even though she would die in less than 12 hours in the hospital, the coroner would probably not want jurisdiction after looking at the CT scan. The nursing administrator would have the chore of notifying his office. Through the years, I've gotten on a first name basis with most of the coroner's investigators.

I dictated my note and then went to look for Bannister. He was having coffee in the break room, which was littered with old pizza boxes, paper coffee cups, old magazines, and some scrubs thrown across the battered chairs and table. He said, "I thought the other one could wait. He's an old guy with diabetes and heart disease, who had a cardiac arrest in the car on the freeway. The wife grabbed the wheel and stopped the car and called 911 on her cell phone. The state cops were 3 minutes away and they hauled him out and started CPR but it was another 8 minutes till the paramedics arrived and got an ECG and shocked him. He was pretty blue by then but they got him ventilated and kept him going till they got here. He was in V fib and it took a lot of lidocaine, bicarb and 2 more shocks before we got a stable rhythm. So, total resuscitation time was at least forty minutes. He had some seizure activity, so we loaded him with Dilantin. He's in room 3."

I said, "Thanks, I guess"

Room 3 was the cardiac resuscitation room and was larger than the other rooms except for the trauma bay, which was one large room with six beds. The patient was on the bed, with a nurse watching the monitor and the IV fluids. There were three intravenous lines running, one for Lidocaine, another for dopamine to support his blood pressure and the last for fluid support. He had been intubated, and the respiratory tech was adjusting the ventilator. The old man was obese, probably 250 lbs, and his feet were mottled blue. About every 30 seconds, he would have a slight body twitch and his eyes would open and roll up. The twitch was making the techs job more difficult as each twitch triggered the ventilator, but when he was still, there were no spontaneous breathing movements. When I touched him, a flurry of twitches followed. His pupils were dilated and did not react to light, nor did they move on moving his head from side to side. Every neurologist who works in a hospital would have recognized post- anoxic seizures and would know the awful prognosis they predict. The old man would likely never wake up if he survived at all. The cardiologists would try to fix his heart but there was no fixing the brain which was in its death throes. I ordered an additional anti-seizure drug and an EEG for the morning. I knew the seizures would eventually stop even without drugs when the damaged neurons finally died. He would be moved to the coronary care unit, and hang round for a few days while the family gathered and hoped until it was obvious to them that there was no hope. I would be called on to talk with the family, tell them what they probably already knew and get their consent to withdraw support. Then the usual orders for comfort care. Without support, most post-arrest patients did not last a day. I sometimes tell my friends "If I'm found down, walk away and have a beer, then come back and call the coroner." They think I'm joking.

With a modest break, I thought that I should go to ICU and start to work out why Sarah was almost completely paralyzed. From the ED it's a short walk to the large elevator to ICU. St. James has basically three ICUs, one mainly for trauma, a medical ICU and the large cardiac and cardiovascular surgery unit. Sarah was in the trauma ICU because the medical unit was full. The trauma ICU has 20 beds in one large room with groups of two or three beds served by a mini-nursing station. Each bed was in its own cubicle and can be isolated in case of air transmitted infection.

As I looked through her chart, I recalled that there had been something unusual about the intubation process. With a rapidly acting neuromuscular blocking agent like succinylcholine, the drug usually induces muscle twitching because it releases acetylcholine as it depolarizes the neuromuscular junction. Sarah had not twitched, which meant to me that either the release of the transmitter from the nerve side of the muscle –nerve junction was blocked, or that the receptors on the muscle side were blocked or destroyed. This meant either botulism or myasthenia gravis. It was less likely to be Guillian –Barre, a disease in which the motor nerves are damaged because in that condition, the weakness comes on over a week or more. I ordered blood tests for the presence of botulinum toxin and for antibodies to the acetylcholine receptor but I knew those would take over a week to get back and I would get as much information from electrical studies and from talking to her and her family.

I was standing at the nursing station outside of her cubicle with the chart when I noticed that she was watching me through her half-closed eyes. There had not been much time to examine her in the ED and it was too dark in the MRI.

It was time for a more formal introduction. I went to the bedside and said "I'm Dr. ----------, I'm a neurologist and I'd like to ask you some questions. I ask them so that you can answer yes or no by nodding or shaking your head OK?" Nod.

"Have you eaten any home canned food?" Shake.

"Has anyone at home or at work been sick?" Shake.

"Have you had the flu or diarrhea recently?" Shake.

"Have you had any other problems like this prior to last week?" Nod.

"Was the problem double vision?" Nod

Her shakes and nods were becoming weaker and I had enough information for now. My exam was somewhat limited. Her eyelids were partially closed, the right was lower. Both pupils reacted to light and were equal. The eyes were dysconjugate, with the right drifted out and the left down. The conjunctiva were moist, indicating that she was capable of making tears. She had only minimal facial movement, but did manage a weak smile. Her limbs were weak but there was no sign of atrophy and her knee reflexes were present but vanished on repeated testing. She seemed to be in good overall physical condition, with only minimal signs of her age. I remember being struck by two thoughts, one was that she seemed somehow familiar, and the other was that I wished we had met under other circumstances.

I took her hand and said "I'll go and talk with your family. I think this is treatable and we will get started tomorrow." She gave my hand a weak squeeze.

I was very suspicious that this petite, ash-blond gray-eyed lady had myasthenia gravis and while this was treatable, she was in for a long haul.

I met her son and daughter in the ICU waiting room and learned that she was 45 years old, divorced, not remarried and with no significant other. She lived with her son and daughter in a two-story home, also housing a tortoise shell cat. She was an executive in a resort.

She had no significant illness, no allergies, took prescribed valproic acid, would only drink with friends and did not smoke. The bare bones of a person.

Chapter 3

I think it takes a certain amount of boldness to be a physician, to think that with a certain amount of knowledge and some pharmacology you can save a life or restore function. Hubris, I think the Greeks called it. Sure, part of this is put on, as confidence in the doctor inspires confidence in the patient. Some of this confidence is born of experience but most is due to ignorance, not knowing what we don't know. I felt fairly certain that once the diagnosis was made in Sarah's case, that therapy would put her back on her feet and back to her life. Ignorance of the future is a gift, I suppose, because otherwise we would despair or not try at all.

Finishing out the rest of the day's consults and rounds at nineteen hundred, I was planning the next step in the diagnostic process, namely electrical study of her nerves and muscles. That would involve moving the EMG machine from its lair in the bowels of the hospital to the ICU and then finding an electrical outlet that had a minimum of 60 cycle electrical interference. When trying to measure electrical currents in the microvolt range, it doesn't take much radiofrequency noise to screw things up. When I started my training, this equipment was barely out of the vacuum tube stage.

Now it is run by a laptop computer and the direct coupled amplifiers have digital filters.

After I had hauled the EMG machine up to ICU and found an outlet that did not have a lot of 60 cycle hum in the amplifiers, I walked over to Sarah's bed and tried to explain the procedure. "Ms. Smith, I'm going to do some testing that will involve stimulating the nerves in your arms or legs with some electricity. The shock feels like this" I tapped her forearm sharply with my fingertip. "It is not like sticking your finger in a wall socket. I probably will need to stick a small needle into some of your muscles. I'll try to keep that to a minimum. Can I proceed?" Her eyes opened slightly and she nodded.

So much for informed consent. I coated two disc electrodes with conductive gel and taped them to the little finger side of her left hand. I put a gel coated ground electrode on the palm side of her wrist and put the stimulating electrode over the site of the ulnar nerve just above her wrist crease. I turned up the stimulator voltage to where I thought I would get a response and hit the trigger. A waveform appeared on the screen and the readout showed 5 millivolts and 3.5 milliseconds latency. The size of the wave was a little low, so I tuned up the voltage another 25 volts and hit the trigger. This time the time was the same but the readout showed 3.2 millivolts. I thought that I had moved the stimulator off the nerve, so I repositioned it and hit the trigger again. This time the readout showed 2.7 millivolts. It was clear that my technique was good and the dropping wave amplitude was due to a neuromuscular conduction block, either myasthenia gravis or botulism or a similar problem.

Since the junction fails at high stimulus frequencies, I was able to get the nerve conduction study done by stimulating at 30 to 45 second intervals and was able to establish that her nerves alone were intact. Now it was time to go back and figure out what kind of neuromuscular block she had. Myasthenia and botulism give different patterns of responses depending on the stimulus frequency. A decreasing response with a slow 2 per second stimulus and no increased response after exercise is typical of myasthenia gravis. So I reset the electrodes to the little finger side of her hand, and taped a stimulating electrode to the wrist over the ulnar nerve and then taped her fingers together. The EMG machine has a setting to determine the optimum stimulus before doing the testing. That took about a minute, and then I let her hand rest for about 2 minutes. While waiting, I talked to her about the results so far, she watched me with eyes partially close and her head tilted trying to reduce the double vision. Occasionally she would nod and try to smile.

Test time. I hit the trigger, and the stimulator fired nine times and the recorder printed out the result. The drop in amplitude from the first to the fourth stimulus was 60 percent and the drop to the ninth was seventy percent. I asked her to try to spread her fingers apart against the tape restraint for twenty seconds, as I watched the second hand of my watch. I said "OK, relax, here is another series."

I hit the trigger again and watched the screen as the traces appeared. There was no increase in amplitude and the decrease from first to fourth was even worse. I waited two minutes and repeated the series. There was no improvement. I was convinced that she had myasthenia gravis and that with medication and some time she would be back on her feet.

.

I said, "Ms. Smith, I think this is myasthenia, which is a condition in which the nerves do not transmit to your muscles. With medication, we should be able to get your strength back and get that tube out of your throat. I'll get the orders written and start tonight"

I took the tape and electrodes off her hand and then noticed some tears. I got some tissue and wiped the tears and then brushed the hair off her face. I stared at her for a moment, thinking that she was terribly composed. I had been hospitalized once for an infection that damn near killed me, but I had never been awake, paralyzed and intubated and unable to communicate. She either had a tremendous faith or an iron will. I said "I have to go, I'll be back first thing in the morning." She gave me a faint smile, possibly the only facial movement she could manage. I returned the EMG machine to its home in the basement and went back to the ICU.

At the nursing station, I pulled up a stool and sat to write my orders and glancing up saw that she was looking at me from half closed eyes. I wrote for intravenous steroids, strong anti-inflammatory medication, to be started, along with some tube feeding, so she would get the necessary calories and protein to prevent bone and muscle loss from the steroids. I ordered a Tensilon® (edrophonium chloride) test for morning to confirm the diagnosis. This drug preserves the neurotransmitter at the nerve- muscle junction, and if there is a definite increase in strength, longer acting versions of the same class can be used long term.

The pager had gone off several times while I was working with Sarah, and I started to return the calls. One was from the ED and the clerk said Dr. Bannister was tied up and had left word to try back in fifteen minutes. Most of the other calls were from the neurology/ neurosurgery ward, where most of my patients and those of the five physicians whose practice I was covering were housed. Most of the problems were routine. One needed a sleeper; another had spiked a fever and needed blood studies, a chest X-ray and cultures of blood and urine. Still another needed something to get her bowels moving. Long experience had taught me to get these minor things settled before I went home or the nurses would never let me get some sleep. Bannister's clerk said he might give me fifteen minutes.

No such luck. Bannister was on the phone five minutes later, with a story about a lady with a headache. He didn't want to let her go home without a check, lest he miss something that would come back and bite him in the butt. The rule is if you can shift the blame, do so. I walked back down the stairs and down the hall to the ED. The usual maelstrom of noise hit me as I walked through the automatic doors with my pass card. Intercom blaring, phones ringing, beeping IV pumps and the constant moaning, screaming, sobbing of people in rooms, in the hallway, family members, cops, orderlies, nurses and physicians milling in seeming random motion.

Bannister said, "She is in room three. He husband is with her and somewhat hostile. We got the CT done but she has been here five hours because of the trauma cases. I almost called security before he calmed down. The social worker gave him a cafeteria pass"

I tapped on the door and then slid the door back to enter. The lights were dimmed, suggesting to me that she was photophobic. The gurney was directly in front of me and the husband was sitting on a chair off to the left. My light adapted eyes could just make out shapes initially. He stood up as the door slid back and as my eyes adjusted, I could make out a huge man, easily six foot four in a sleeveless T shirt, jeans, boots and enough tattoos to impress a Hells Angel. Some of the tattoos were of prison quality.

The patient could wait a moment. The first priority was to deal with the husband. I extended my hand saying "Sir, I'm Dr. ---------. I'm sorry you have been waiting so long. The ED doctor just told me about your wife. I've been told the CT scan is normal. Let me talk to her for a moment and examine her and then I'll talk with both of you"

"OK doc". He replied.

I asked "Ma'am do you have headaches a lot?"

She said, "Sure do, at least once a month, but this was a bad one, but it's mostly gone now.'

I asked "Do they follow your menstrual periods?"

She said "Yeah. They start on the second day, but I never had loss of vision before this"

I asked "Can you see now?

She replied "I couldn't see for about ten minutes, and then the headache started on the left side of my head behind my eye."

My next question "Who else in the family gets headaches?"

She said "My mother used to get them, and my sister still does."

Her carotid arteries in the neck were normal. Her blood pressure was normal. Through the opthalmoscope the quick view of her retina looked normal. I smelled a faint odor of cigarette smoke but could not tell from which person it came.

I asked her "Do you smoke or take birth control pills?

She said "Yeah, I've been on birth control for two years to regulate my periods. But I don't smoke more than half a pack a day."

I said "Well, I think the headaches are migraines and that was what caused your temporary loss of vision. But I need to tell you that even though you're twenty-six, the smoking and birth control meds raise your risk of stroke substantially and I would recommend stopping one or the other and preferably both; the smoking especially as that raises your risk for heart attack as well. If both of you stop, it might be easier. There are some new medications that can stop your headache if taken early enough, and your family doctor can discuss those with you. If he can't help you, give me a call. Here's my card."

The big guy stuck out a hand the size of a dinner plate and said "Thanks doc. I sure appreciate it". A soft answer turns away wrath.

I took one last walk through ICU but Sarah seemed to be asleep. Time to head home and feed the dogs. I might sleep, I might not. The house is lonely with your mother gone. You might think that as I was an only child, I might be used to loneliness. Well, it doesn't seem to work that way. I think there is a greater need for human contact in only children, which may explain why I left the research labs and later a drug company to return to practice and why I feel most alive when seeing patients.

CHAPTER 4

Well Kathleen, that's how this drama started. As you know now from clinical experience, the initial days of any patient's admission are a spasm of diagnostic and therapeutic procedures followed by clinical observation for improvement or not. Everything begins with some certainty and not a little hope. The next two months were to see the unraveling of both which thankfully I could not foresee. Nor could I foresee the effect this chance encounter would have on both of us.

The next day, Saturday, the phone and beeper were quiet and I had the whole morning to catch up on admissions and consults. I went to ICU to see Sarah first. It had been about twelve hours since I had started the steroid infusion, and I hoped there was some benefit. The nurses had combed her hair and brushed her teeth and she seemed to be happy to see me. Her eyes were more open, her smile a little broader and I imagined her grip was slightly better. I explained that I would do the Tensilon® test to confirm the diagnosis and how it would work. She nodded in agreement.

The nurses had prepared the two syringes, one of atropine to block the Tensilon effect on her heart, and the drug in the other. Tensilon blocks the breakdown of acetylcholine, the neurotransmitter at the nerve muscle junction and the increase in the chemical allows more strength in contraction. I needed a clear endpoint to be sure I was right in my diagnosis. The easiest thing would be to measure the width of her eyelid opening. I got a clear plastic ruler from the nursing station and held it just in front of each eye. The right was two millimeters, the left three. I injected the atropine into the IV line, gave it about thirty seconds to circulate, then began to inject the Tensilon.

I asked "Ms. Smith, please look at the sound of my voice, even if you can't see me"

After the first two milligrams had been injected, I glanced at the monitor to be sure she was not developing any cardiac slowing, and then injected the remaining eight milligrams. After about thirty seconds, her eyelids began to lift and I was greeted by the sight of beautiful gray eyes in perfect alignment and the beginnings of a real smile. I can't remember whose smile was bigger. I was impressed. Despite the ET tube and nasogastric tube, she had a radiance that beautiful women possess no matter the circumstances.

The drug effect lasts less than five minutes and shortly the smile faded and eyelids drooped. A tear appeared.

I said "Ms. Smith, the test was positive and I'll start a long acting version of the drug through the NG tube. It will take a few days to get the dose adjusted. I'd like to get a CT scan of your chest to see if there is an enlargement of your thymus gland, which can sometimes provoke myasthenia. "

I took her hand and said "Try not to worry, once the drugs start to work, we should be able to get the tubes out and get you out of here." I got a slight squeeze in reply.

Back at the nursing station, I wrote orders for the CT scan and to start pyridostigmine down the NG tube. I reviewed the labs, noting that none of the acetylcholine receptor antibody tests were back, nor were the botulinum toxin studies. The botulinum toxin test goes to the Centers for Disease Control (CDC) who are generally reluctant to run the tests without definite clinical evidence of botulism. The lab had left a note in the pending file that a conference call with the CDC was scheduled. I had not expected fast results and felt comfortable with the data so far. Nevertheless, I found myself glancing down the nursing station to her room, wishing I could see her smile again

Just then, Jim Davidson, one of the pulmonary specialists, tapped me on the shoulder and motioned me into a side room where he said "Mac, I need your help with a delicate matter. There is a guy in pod three next to your lady, who shot himself in the head two months ago, and then had a respiratory arrest on the ward, and probably sustained some more brain damage. He's been in ICU for a month on the vent and has not shown much progress. I'd like you to take a look and give us a prognosis so we can decide what to tell the family"

I said "OK I'll see him today. But is there something else I should know?"

He replied "Yeah, but you'll see that when you review the chart"

I finished Sarah's orders and then walked to the next station to find the patient's chart which was in three volumes which is not a good sign. I started with the history and physical at the back of the current volume. The admitting physician was a trauma surgeon and there were consults from the ear, nose and throat specialists as well as pulmonary medicine, internal medicine, neurosurgery, psychiatry and rehabilitation medicine.

The story was strange and I quickly understood why Davidson had not wanted to talk in front of the nurses. Apparently the guy was intoxicated and arguing with his wife with the children present. To make a point, he pulled out a snub-nose .38 caliber revolver and stuck the barrel in his mouth. Now I'm not suggesting you try this, but it's pretty hard to hold the barrel straight and level and pointed at the back of your throat where the bullet would pass through the brainstem and take you out quickly. He either dropped his hand or the recoil tipped the barrel up and as a result the bullet went straight up through his palate, blew away the sphenoid and maxillary sinuses, took out a piece of the left frontal lobe of his brain and exited through the top of his skull. I guess he made his point to his wife but he also made a mess and a hell of a problem for the doctors. The big and continuing problem was maintaining his airway. The neurosurgeons had patched up the hole in the bottom of the skull where the bullet entered the brain and stopped the leak of cerebrospinal fluid, but there was not much that could be done for the sinuses, and there was continual drainage of blood, pus, and mucus into his airway. They finally put in a tracheostomy so that air went directly into the trachea which was sealed off from the damaged oropharyx. He stabilized after that, enough to be transferred to the medical ward and there Davidson's problem really began.

As you know from growing up around here, the Great Basin region has about the same geography and climate as the Gobi desert. Not many people want to live here unless they grew up here or are semi-voluntary exiles like myself. You have to like vast distances and the color brown. That makes it hard to recruit nurses, and so the hospital hires nurses from agencies, sometimes at extravagant rates. Some are very good and others are simply mercenaries and like the mercenaries hired by the Italian city states have loyalty only to their paycheck. Well, it was late at night, about shift change, and when report was given, someone got tired of hearing his pulse oximeter/ apnea monitor go off and turned off the alarm. Report must have taken some time, probably because it included discussion of last night's date or hair styles. By the time the oncoming nurse made her rounds he was quite blue from a mucus plug obstructing his airway. They called a code and resuscitated him, to no apparent purpose, as he never woke up.

Clearly this was an embarrassment for the hospital, and a potential liability if the family knew about it and made an issue. Legally, a brain injured patient who requires constant care is worth a lot more to a plaintiff's attorney than one who is already dead. My problem was to determine whether he was in a vegetative state and get the family to make a decision regarding his care. I would have to tell them what had happened in some form and wait to see if the wanted to know about negligence.

Diagnosis of vegetative state is based on history of illness and mostly, repeated detailed clinical observation. I went to the bedside and looked him over. His eyes were open but he did not seem to respond to my entrance. He yawned. I walked over and looked in his face – no interest evident. I rapidly thrust my index finger toward his right eye- no blink. Left eye was the same. I yelled his name-no response. I pinched the skin over his nipple between my fingernails- no response. After this test, I looked at the ECG monitor- his heart rate had not changed. His arms and legs had normal muscle tone. Reflexes were equal from side to side. The pupils of both eyes were equal and constricted to light. When I turned his head to the right, both eyes drifted to the left. I left the room and went back to the chart. The nurses had not noted any sign of awareness, and from their notes, he did not respond to his family. I paged back through the three volumes and could see that from the respiratory arrest on the ward, that these responses or lack of response had been stable for the last month.

Except for the fact that the time since his respiratory arrest was less than three months ago, he fit the neurologic criteria for persistent vegetative state. I wrote a brief note documenting my findings and ordered a CT scan of his head and an EEG. I didn't leave an impression pending the tests and a discussion with the family. The nurses said that they had not been in during the last few days.

Persistent vegetative state is a bit of a problem for neurologists. The definition is no problem as it is state of no awareness of the environment or family despite apparent wakefulness. The victims often have intact brainstem function, respiration, swallowing, and eye movements and sleep wake cycles. Most criteria require there to be no change for at least three months. Most such patients are victims of hypoxia or lack of blood flow due to cardiac arrest. Most eventually die, but rarely one will improve slightly. The problem is how do you know they have no awareness? Lack of external response is often the only evidence although sometimes EEG will help, especially if the waves do not change in response to a strong stimulus. Somewhere between this state and full responsiveness is a vague condition called minimally responsive state, in which the patient has occasional, low level responses to some stimuli but not all. Recently , in this latter group sophisticated MRI imaging techniques have show some brain network response to a loved ones voice or a favorite piece of music, even though the patient had no external response.

Most often in the clinic or at the bedside we rely on what we can see and available evidence about outcomes in similar cases. Medicine is after all, a game of probability. Once I had the test results, I would meet with the family, try to generate a defensible prognosis and then lay out their options.

Saturday afternoon passed in a continuous stream of phone calls, consults and talks with staff physicians and residents. Before I went home, I walked through the ICU to check with the nurses about Sarah. They said she was stable and I left it at that. I got about four hours sleep Saturday night before the phone calls started again. It seems that there is usually a break in emergencies about three AM and I recall, as interns, we would get wheelchairs and roll them out on the ambulance dock and tilt them back to gaze at the stars for a brief moment of peace.

Sunday morning used to be a family time with Mass and a leisurely breakfast and the Sunday paper. Now it is just another day with less traffic to deal with. I started hospital rounds across town and, with interruptions, did not get to St James until afternoon. Sarah seemed to be sleeping and that was probably due to the sedation the pulmonary physicians order to relieve anxiety and keep patients from fighting the respirator. I didn't try to wake her but sat by the bedside while I reviewed the chart. I think I just wanted a break in the work, but also, in retrospect, I think I was getting some sense of peace being near her. I only spent about five minutes at the bedside before being paged away. She was still on my mind when I was at home some hours later. I knew that I had more emotional investment in this case than in the others from the weekend and that was a bit troubling. A little more balance was desirable. That could wait till morning.

I was off call on Monday and had a fairly busy schedule. It was time to head to the clinic for the morning's work. First, though I wanted to walk by Sarah's room. With a quick look from a distance, I couldn't see any big difference, certainly not the dramatic improvement I had seen with the Tensilon. Well, I thought it could be just a matter of dose adjustment and time for the steroids to work. It was not uncommon for steroids to transiently worsen myasthenia gravis, before the disease came under control. I would need more time to see if the medications were working, and maybe to see that smile again. As I passed by, I reminded myself that the endotracheal tube could be in place for only a week or so before the cuff on the end of the tube that seals the trachea would start to erode through the tissue. Before that, she would need a tracheostomy, a surgical procedure to put a tube directly in the trachea with a cuff that could be deflated from time to time.

CHAPTER FIVE

The clinic work was the usual follow –up appointments for Parkinson's disease and dementia with a new patient consult for headaches thrown in just before lunch. At lunch time, I reviewed the CT scan on the gunshot victim with the radiologist. There was some artifact due to surgical clips and small particles of bullet, but the cortex was very thin and shrunken and the brain cavities were dilated in response to the loss of brain tissue. Clearly, this guy was not going back to reading the Wall Street Journal. The EEG was an unvarying slow rhythm about two cycles per second which did not change when the technician called his name, pinched him or flashed light in his eyes. Even the usual EEG response to repeated flashes of light was absent. I now had all the data I needed and called the ICU nursing station to set up the family conference for morning. I didn't think the patient was ever going to be any more aware than he was now and it remained for the family and their advisors to give us some direction. I had no idea of his religious beliefs if any and even less those of his family. Tomorrow would be an interesting exploration.

The EEG on the cardiac arrest patient from Friday night showed a burst suppression pattern, bursts of epileptic discharges separated by periods of flat line tracing. Most patients with this pattern die and the ones that don't, never awaken. I went up to the CCU and walked through the double doors. The unit is U shaped with a central nursing and monitoring station. The patient list is on a white board near the utility room, listing the room number and the nurse responsible. I looked through the chart while the nurse worked with the patient next door. The room was empty save for the patient, IV pumps and one old, thin, white haired woman sitting next to the window, staring at the bed and turning a handkerchief over and over in her hand.

On the front of the chart was a welcome sight, the patient's advance directive which his wife must have brought from home. It had the usual boiler plate with various options checked. He did not want support if he was irreversibly comatose and appointed his wife as attorney in fact. The cardiologists has stabilized his heart, but the lab data showed he had sustained a massive heart attack and the cardiac ultrasound study showed a heart that had lost eighty percent of its pumping power. His kidneys were failing as was his liver from reduced blood flow. Time was running out.

I went up to her and introduced myself and asked her to leave the room for a moment while I examined him. The seizure activity that I had seen last night was no more. His pupils still did not constrict to light and head rotation did not move the eyes. He did not respond to painful stimulus and his limbs had no muscle tone. I knew she was watching me as I went through the motions of examining him. I could guess how and what she was feeling, a stranger in an alien world of white coats, machines and alarms, a spectator in a drama that was changing, maybe ending the life of the man she had known for over thirty years.

I went back out of the room and met her. The handkerchief was now in a tight white ball, pressed against her lips as if to keep the sorrow from spilling out. She spoke first.

She asked "It's not good is it?

I said "No, his brain is badly damaged, his heart is bad and his kidneys and liver are failing. No matter what we do, he can't go on much longer."

Her voice was breaking as she said "He wasn't feeling well when we left home. I should have made him stay home, but I can't see well enough to drive. And we went right past the hospital before the freeway. And then I couldn't get him out of the car to give him CPR the right way till the troopers arrived."

I said "I read his advance directive that says if he won't recover we are not to keep him going. But you are the one to make the decision. Are there other family members that you can talk with?"

She said "No, his kids haven't spoken to him for years, something to do with his previous marriage."

I asked, "Do you have any family here to talk to?"

She said "No, my sister died two years ago, and my boy died in Vietnam thirty years ago. My husband is all I have left and he is going now isn't he?"

I said "Yes, now or in a day or two. If it's any consolation, he is not suffering now. "

She said "I know but it's still hard to let him go. There's nothing left. Just a void. I can't decide now."

I said "OK, I understand, but we need some guidance about what to do if his heart stops tonight. Do we shock him back like the paramedics did?"

She replied "No, I don't want that. If he has a new heart attack tonight, that's it. Maybe that's for the best."

I said "OK, I'll write a no code order. The rest of his care will be unchanged. I'll be by tomorrow and we'll talk again." There was a pause as we looked at each other, then she turned away.

She went back into the room and sat down and resumed staring at him. I went back to the chart and wrote the orders. I've learned over the years that families have to be guided into decisions they know are necessary but hate to make. Sometimes it's a race between the failing biology and the gradually building family consensus.

I had about twenty minutes before I was due back at the office. I went back to ICU to check on Sarah, because I was becoming concerned that the drugs were not as effective as I had hoped. She must have sensed my standing outside her room flipping through the chart. She was tipping her head back to see beyond her lowered eyelids. Her lung function studies showed not much improvement in her chest and diaphragm muscle strength, at least not enough to support life. I increased the pryidostigmine dose by fifty percent. I went to her bedside and took her hand.

I said "Ms. Smith, I'm increasing the medication, and you might get some cramping sensation in your abdomen. If this is not enough to enable you to breath on your own, I'll try plasmaphoresis, which is a procedure where we take off blood, remove the plasma and the antibodies causing your weakness and give back the cells. I'll know by tomorrow if I will need to do this. If I do I will have to have a surgeon implant some tubes in the veins for vascular access. Do you understand?"

I got a brief nod and a hand squeeze as a response. I pulled up a chair and sat down at the side of the bed and took her hand again. I'm not sure why, possibly to comfort her but just as likely to be with her for a bit. After a minute or two, I said "I want you to know that I'll do the best I can for you, but if you want or your family wants another neurologist to take over, I'll arrange it." She shook her head and wrapped her fingers around my hand.

I said "Right, then we'll push on. I'll be back this evening."

The rest of the afternoon's clinic went smoothly, my office manager was her usual sour self, bemoaning the phone calls, the insurance companies, the flaky copy machine, the no-pay patients, and whatever else was irritating her that day other than me. We had been irritating each other for fifteen years since I had hired her away from another group. Why she came and why she stayed remains a mystery to me. She called me when her husband died suddenly, to deal with the coroner. After five years of widowhood, she met and married an old family friend. She was more than an employee and more than a friend. She watches my back and I trust her completely.

She handles all the practice's finances, deals with the insurance companies and the billing service. Seeing us interact, more than one patient has mistaken her for my wife. I know she has better judgement than that.

It has been my practice to round on critical patients twice a day, mostly because it saves late night phone calls. I walked through CCU, looked in on the old man and noted that his wife was no longer at his bedside. I wondered if that meant that she had made up her mind. In ICU, the nurses told me the family conference was set for nine in the morning with the small ICU conference room reserved. The subject of the conference had not changed and there was a note in the chart from the pulmonary group that I was to write all further orders.

Sarah's lung function studies and CT scan were in the chart. Her breathing ability was not much better and her chest CT was normal, meaning no thymus tumor or enlargement. I went to her bedside to see if her eyes were more open, but could not see a major improvement. I said "I think I'll need to begin the plasmaphoresis as you're not getting better fast enough. I'll call the surgeons to put the lines in tomorrow. Is that OK with you?"

She nodded and reached for my hand. I bent down near her head and said "I think this treatment is going to take a while, at least a week before we can think about getting the breathing tube out." The nurses had left a yellow legal pad and a ball point pen on her bed. She groped for the pen. I put it in her hand and held the pad so she could see it with her head tipped back. Her grip on the pen was weak but she scratched out "Don't quit-don't leave."

As you know, Kathleen, I don't like to take care of myasthenic patients. They are too unpredictable when the disease is extensive. Any little thing, a cold, electrolyte imbalance, a change in medications and with no warning, they are choking on their saliva and gasping for breath. For me, a patient with a stroke or rapidly worsening neuropathy is easier to manage. My colleagues seem to have better luck, or maybe they don't talk about their failures. I suppose that's why I was hinting that she could get someone else. She was having none of that. Patients can fire their doctors for any reason or none at all. Doctors can fire patients for only a few reasons such as non-compliance or threats. I might have argued that I was incompetent for this problem, but in that case there was the option of a second opinion.

Whether she realized it or not, I was left with the moral obligation to see this through. So, we were bound together for a time, one old man and one sick lady. I later thought was it random chance or Providence that I was on call when she was admitted. I don't understand a world where chance rules. I do understand in a limited way, chaos theory, that a seemingly inconsequential event can change a history, driving a universe where choice matters but the results are not readily predictable.

I stood there for a moment and then said goodnight, and went to the nurse's station to make the calls to the surgeons and kidney specialists that direct the plasmaphoresis treatment.

I walked out of the hospital to the parking ramp. Snow was falling, a bit early for October. In a corner of the ramp, the wind swirled up a coil of aspen leaves, mixed with snow. Before the storm, high winds had swept through the valley, stripping away the last of the aspen and maple leaves, leaving only bare and brittle sticks. On other days, I would have looked forward to winter, the bare hills shining in the setting sun, cutting out early on Friday afternoon to take you and your friends skiing, skis and boots and giggling girls piled into the truck for the long run up the mountain. I never cared for alpine skiing as you did. I much preferred to be alone on the high meadow, backpack and cross- country skis and the silence. Well, no more. After your injury, I couldn't drag you to a mountain, and after your mother left, I have too much silence. I know that it was after that injury and the extensive reconstructive surgery that you decided on a career in medicine. But consider our home. Dinner table conversation was mostly medicine and science, your mother, sister, father, aunt and uncle were all in the medical or nursing professions. It's like growing up in a mafia family. Of course you will enter the family business.

I didn't grow up in that kind of environment. I think children do not understand their parents because they never see the genetics or the events in their parents' lives that shaped their character. Did not the Greeks say character is fate? To get to the genetics, I have to go back a generation or two.

You never knew my father, your grandfather. He died thirteen years before you were born. But to see him clearly, you have to go back one more generation to your great grandfather. He was born in the west of Ireland, and worked on an estate, where he met a young woman. They wanted to marry, but the estate owner refused, fearing he would lose a good housemaid. Telling an Irishman how to run his life is unwise. They both emigrated to America and ended up in the hard coal regions of northeastern Pennsylvania where they had kin. He worked on the railroad, probably one of the most dangerous jobs in the area, second only to the underground mines. They were wrapped in the arms of the Church and were part of their fraternal organizations. Baptisms, First Communions, marriages and funerals kept the community together.

The Irish by nature are not a peaceful folk. The large mining companies and the railroads were not enlightened employers. Thus there arose an offshoot of the Ancient Order of Hibernians that struck back at the giant firms, ostensibly to protect the workers. Mining equipment was burned, foremen threatened and occasionally killed. They were part of the early labor union movement but some of their operations were simply for profit by extortion. I recall a Sunday afternoon drive that passed a five foot by ten foot plot at the roadside, bordered by a low, white picket fence and two crosses. I was told that that was the spot where a mine supervisor and his wife were ambushed and murdered.

The gang was known as the Molly Maguires, and they were infiltrated by the Pinkertons, and were arrested and most were hung. One man maintained his innocence and wrote his name in blood on the prison yard wall and swore if he was unjustly executed, the name would remain .He was hung with the rest of the gang and the name remained visible despite paint, whitewash and plaster. The warden finally had the wall demolished and rebuilt.

The point of this history is that the only way out of the mines was through the school house door. And so my father went to college, in a day when there were no student loans or grants. How he did it I'll never know, nor what it cost him. From some brief comments, I know he had some acquaintance with military service, but missed World War 1. He went on to a Masters degree, which was in English. His thesis was a study of Irish lyric poetry, which was the title of a course he taught. I was unaware of this until, in one of our moves, I came across a box with his degree and the thesis and course syllabus. I think this was his first college teaching job. He began his doctoral studies in psychology while teaching.

He taught at the same Catholic university that I attended years later. A lot of the old brick buildings were still there, sitting on the bluff above the river. It was the only place where you could throw a half brick, otherwise known as Irish confetti, five hundred feet. I don't know how he lived through those long years, as the Depression began probably in the middle of his research. I think he lived pretty much as I did during the long years of medical and graduate school, odd jobs, teaching, washing glassware in a lab, living alone in anonymous rooming houses, sometimes with transient roommates but mostly alone. In those Depression days, money was always short. There was a tale that when faculty payday came, the old priest who was the president of the university, would take an old black valise and walk downtown to the law offices and municipal buildings where the alumni, whose careers were based on the education provided by that little university and its night law school, would be persuaded to donate yet again.

38

It was not a life, but a life postponed.

Somehow he survived the Depression, got his degree and found teaching jobs at another Catholic university. He met my mother through her sister who was one of his students. He was forty when I was born, their only child. He missed World War II as he was deemed essential to teach the accelerated officers courses. He became a dean and stayed in the academic arena until he realized that the clergy took a vow of poverty and the faculty kept it. There followed a series of jobs outside the university, some of which were short lived. We moved several times and had a long period when he was unemployed and we lived with relatives. He finally settled into a job in the steel industry where he remained until his retirement. He died a year later. I never knew what he thought about his life. He and my mother were never very demonstrative, but I don't recall any fights or sullen silences. I suppose like many people who lived through the Depression and two world wars, they were happy just to have survived.

I had not realized, until this happened, how similar our lives were a generation apart. Similarities: Well, the long and intense schooling, the general disinterest in athletics except for a fondness for baseball, a love of literature and poetry, and a tendency to be a loner are some common points. A few others, we both married late, and to younger women. There were some differences. I was more interested in the out of doors and hunting and fishing than he. This was supported by my mother's family, one uncle in particular. The other significant difference was that I had more military service and more foreign experience than he, especially in the Far East.

I don't suppose I have to remind you of how intense med school is or how good it feels when you are done for a while. Remember the sense of freedom when you don't have to look forward to the next exam or case presentation or one more hoop to jump through. I know it doesn't last but it's nice for a while. Well that's how my initial military experience was. I helped run a chemistry lab and wrote papers. Regular hours, actual vacations, pleasant people and I got paid! That's where I met your mother. She was a Navy nurse and both of us were enjoying the release from long schooling. I think we both minimized the tension that religious differences impose even when the polarization between her southern Protestant family and my family's northern Catholic culture was evident. It was almost over before it began, until the military chaplain who was a Jesuit and a legend, calmed down the Catholic side.

Military service was for me not a burden, despite the unpleasantness in Southeast Asia at the time. The military research unit where I was assigned studied stress reactions and what better setting for that research than a wartime environment. I was never in serious danger, though there are several experiences that I would not care to repeat. I don't much care for helicopters and I hope I never again have to help pull body parts out of an aircraft air intake. All in all, it was not a bad time for us despite the social turmoil boiling around us. I had, for a time, rediscovered aspects on my faith in an old Spanish mission. I rediscovered the joys of fishing, camping and hiking and learned one more thing. I didn't really want to spend my life toiling in a lab, taking weeks to add points to a graph.

I guess you know that I became a physician almost by accident. I had never considered medical school, even though my undergraduate degree was essentially premed. No one in the family had been in medicine and we were not well off. This was in the days before extensive federal loans were available. When I started my Ph.D. program, the chairman asked me if I ever thought of medical school. Implied was if you get in, we will pay your way. The department had federal money to train medical scientists, people who could cross from the lab to the ward and back again. So, I did and they did and I toiled away for seven years, through several disastrous romances, a bout of depression, and an almost total estrangement from religion. Near the end, I had no idea of what I wanted to do, clinic, lab, both? To keep my options open I did a year of medicine to be eligible for licensure. In the middle of that year the Navy called.

I know it seems that I'm telling this story a bit backwards. But it's important to know that the early years were good. I completed my residency and your mother her master's degree in nursing and I taught at the university for two years before taking a job with a private institute. In only a few years, the promising future began to fade. Good times never last.

CHAPTER 6

The morning ICU conference to review admissions was starting as I arrived in ICU. I presented her case to bring everybody up to date. There were no new ideas. Sarah was still in surgery when the conference had finished. I pulled up her records on the computer and saw that the botulinum toxin studies were back and was negative. This was not a surprise. What was a surprise was that the CDC had responded so quickly. Cases of botulism are rare but the hospital has had three in the last two years and I guess the CDC is getting used to hearing from us.

The snow had closed the main roads in and out of town and the city streets would be impassible for all but four wheel drive trucks with high ground clearance. My office called to let me know not to rush back, as everybody had cancelled. The break would give me a chance to get at some tardy projects, one of which was reviewing research proposals submitted to the hospital. When I came back to practice, the research experience and my familiarity with federal rules regarding research subjects was all the excuse the administration needed to put me on a human subjects committee. This was a good thing in a way, as it spared me from serving on some more politically sensitive committee. Research ethics are simply a branch of medical or bioethics which has lately become a growth industry. Defrocked clergy, under-employed attorneys and academician philosophers write voluminous articles that wind up providing more questions than answers. Physicians make ethical decisions every day, often without thinking about the principles involved.

Modern, secular, medical ethics arose out of the Nuremberg trials of the Nazi physicians who conducted experiments on prisoners in the death camps. Although at first applied to research subjects and incorporated into federal law, the fundamental principles of respect for persons, beneficence and justice have now been expanded to cover all aspects of medical care. Respect for persons is basically patient autonomy, which ranges from the patient's right to informed consent to the right to refuse recommended treatment. Beneficence means we act in the patient's best interest, market forces, hospital priorities and insurance companies notwithstanding. A related concept is non-maleficence, meaning we should avoid or minimize suffering. Justice means we should offer the appropriate treatment to every patient regardless of social or financial status. Justice also implies a social responsibility in the use of social resources.

The principles are often in conflict, just as rights conflict. Freedom of speech excludes the right to incite a riot. When a patient demands a futile, or worse, a harmful treatment, doctors have to decide whether to honor the patient's autonomy or refrain from causing harm. Most of the time, this conflict can be resolved by discussion but sometime the doctor has to sign off the case or let an impartial body such as an ethics committee decide the issue. Conflicts involving justice afflict national health systems more than they trouble our private health system. National health systems, such as England's buy drugs for their citizens with limited amounts of money. The British government has a committee that decides which drugs to purchase based on cost and effectiveness. A cheap but moderately effective drug will make the cut over a very effective but pricey drug. The first part of the equation, cost, is easy. Effectiveness is quite another matter. Drug efficacy studies involve select patients and may not reflect real world practice. Separate studies may yield different results and so may be combined statistically. Here is where bias can enter. First, the doctors doing the analysis are paid by the government and secondly, they already know the results of the studies that are to be combined.

The British committee measures efficacy based on a derived measure called quality adjusted years of life. Basically, if a drug provides a good quality of life over a number of years relative to its cost they will put it on the list to buy. Thus, an expensive drug such as Herceptin® that treats breast cancer in young women will be purchased, but a drug that slightly improves quality of life for an elderly patient with dementia will not. Justice would say that the elderly are discriminated as they subsist on government pensions and are not taxpayers. The British authorities say limited resources mandate their procedure. In fact the committee was accused of ignoring the cost savings that the dementia drugs generate in delaying nursing home placement.

The professional ethicists assume that the physician is a calculating machine, weighing efficacy, cost and appropriateness in deciding therapy with no personal involvement in the process. I know that is not true as my own experience has shown. But how does the physician's personal involvement change the decision process? We have bias, belief, disgust and a lot of other moral judgments that are difficult to acknowledge, in addition to the love and respect we have for our patients some of whom are friends or more than friends. I didn't expect to have a practical application of these concepts that same day.

I made my evening rounds through ICU and saw that Sarah was back from surgery. She was still somewhat sedated and had the Permacath vascular acsess tubing protruding from her neck. Her chart showed that the kidney specialists who would direct the plasmaphoresis had scheduled the first session for morning. Her labs were normal but the acetylcholine receptor antibody studies that I needed to confirm the diagnosis were not back. This was no surprise as I had planned to start the therapy and adjust as data arrived.

I had just about made it out of the unit when Davidson called "Mac, don't leave, come over here. We have a problem in room 15" I turned and saw a crowd of nurses and respiratory therapists at the door to room 15. As I walked to the room, I recalled some details of the case that I had overheard at lunch. The patient was a young pregnant woman, with a viral pneumonia that had rendered her lungs so stiff that only a volume cycled respirator was keeping her alive and that only after she had been sedated and paralyzed with a neuromuscular blocking agent. She was 20 weeks pregnant when she was admitted and now was at 30 weeks, if my recollection was accurate. Davidson caught up with me and supplied then up to date history. "We didn't think we could keep her going much longer, so the OB' s did a C section this afternoon as the fetus was viable and the husband would not agree to an abortion. She has been back in the unit about an hour when she blew a pupil. That occurred at 1600"

It was now 1730. If she had had a stroke, we had only 90 minutes left to use thrombolytic drugs. The main drug we use is known as rTPA for recombinant tissue thromboplastin activator. No wonder we like initials. It attaches to thrombin in blood clots and dissolves the clot. All clots, no matter where. As you have learned, we clot blood and dissolve clots all the time in a balanced process.

Clotting after surgery is vital as the surgeon cannot tie off or ligate every tiny vessel. This young lady had had a cesarean section, which involved an abdominal incision and an incision into the uterus to deliver the baby. I think she had a post-partum stroke either due to amniotic fluid embolus or activation of the clotting process by tissue trauma. In either case, the hospital protocols for the use of rTPA restrict its use to non- postoperative patients, for the simple reason that they will bleed, a lot. Still bleeding is one thing and a brainstem stroke quite another, a stroke that could leave her paralyzed and comatose or dead. Yet her lung disease was so severe that she might not survive, leaving her child without a mother and her husband as a widower.

Time was running out. Still, there was a chance that the blown pupil could simply be a third nerve palsy and not a stroke. Third nerve palsies can occur in diabetes and for no other obvious reason. Since she had been given a neuromuscular blocking agent, there was no physical examination technique that would distinguish a third nerve palsy from a brainstem stroke. The only way to be sure was to do a MRI of the brain, as a CT scan would not detect a stroke in this time frame. I was fairly sure I knew the answer as I asked Davidson "Can we get an MRI done?" He replied "No way. The volume cycled vent can't be in the MRI and the pressure cycled unit won't work. We either do something now or do nothing."

I asked Davidson "How much blood is on call for her?"

He replied "I think the usual two units"

I said "If we use TPA she will bleed a lot. So get the blood here before we start. How much does she weigh?"

He checked the chart. "Last recorded weight was sixty kilos."

I noticed the ICU pharmacist filling a drug dispenser and waved her over. She was a jolly middle-aged lady working on her doctorate in pharmacy and had probably forgotten more about drug kinetics and interactions than I ever knew. I briefly told her what Davidson and I were considering.

She looked at me and said "You've got to be kidding. If it's an amniotic fluid embolus it won't work and she will bleed profusely and might die from shock. If the stroke is in the brainstem, she might bleed into the site and die."

"You got a better idea?"

A pause "No"

I said "Well, she is sixty kilos, so at point nine milligrams per kilo we'll need fifty four milligrams, and the NIH protocol calls for ten percent push and the rest over an hour."

She said somewhat testily "I know the protocol; I just hope this doesn't turn into a disaster"

She went to the unit pharmacy to prepare the rTPA and returned with the small vial and a cart with extra iv bags, a pressure infuser , bottles of calcium gluconate and a collection of various other drugs that she had picked off the pharmacy shelves just in case.

Her tension made me want to lighten the scene, so I said "You must have been a Boy Scout."

She was having none of that. "Yeah, right. If this works you will owe me."

She passed the TPA solution to the nurse, who plugged it into one of the two IV lines that were already in place. One of these was a central line, which is long IV tubing that had been threaded through an arm vein into the vena cava, the main vein leading to the heart. The ten percent rTPA bolus went into the central line. I stepped to the head of the bed to see if the eye changed. Nothing much happened for about ten minutes.

Then the pupil started to constrict. And it reacted to light. I was about to give a sigh of relief when the nurse at the foot of the bed said "We've got a bit of bleeding here."

"Where?", I asked.

She said "Vaginal and I take that back, we've got quite a lot of bleeding here"

I asked "How much?"

Briefly ,"Gushing."

Davidson ordered the nurse to hang the blood and turn up the IV rate to two hundred ccs per hour.

Another nurse reported "Her pressure is dropping, now 100 over 60"

Davidson ordered a dopamine drip to keep the systolic pressure above 120, and called for an additional two units of blood. One of the aides went running to the blood bank to get the blood while another took the last unit on hand, hooked it onto the central line and wrapped a blood pressure cuff around the blood bag and pumped it up to 30. I hoped the central line would hold the pressure.

I asked the nurse "How much bleeding did you have before the TPA started?"

She replied "Just a pad an hour"

The pharmacist returned with the dopamine and said "We have got to stop the bleeding. How about giving some ergotamine?"

Ergotamine can constrict blood vessels, but is a potent uterine muscle stimulant and if the uterus contracted the bleeding might stop or at least slow down. It also constricts cerebral and coronary vessels and could cause a myocardial infarction or worsen her stroke. In for a penny, in for a pound.

I told her to give the standard dose. She had it ready in a syringe.

She handed the syringe to the nurse who pushed it into a port in the line.

I asked the pharmacist "How fast does this stuff work?"

She said "Couple of minutes."

I looked at the clock above the bed. We had been at this for an hour.

I asked the nurse at the foot of the bed "How are you doing down there?"

She replied "The bleeding looks like it's slowing down a bit "

I stepped around to the side of the bed to see what she was talking about. This nurse was a master of under statement. The whole end of the bed was soaked with blood, it was dripping onto the floor, and they had been using towels, sheets and pads to try to keep up. The aide bringing the two units from the blood bank slipped in the gore and nearly dropped both blood bags. The nurses matched the numbers and hung the first unit and had the aide squeeze the bag in both hands to speed delivery.

The patient's blood pressure started to climb slightly, and Davidson backed down the dopamine drip. With the third unit running, and the fourth ready, I thought we were getting ahead. If the bleeding could be controlled, we could replace the red cells and fluids faster than she could lose them.

"Oh shit. She's bleeding again" the nurse at the foot of the bed had panic in her voice. I could see the pads and sheet turning crimson again. The pharmacist said "Uterine atony" meaning basically that the muscle cells had quit contracting and was not responding to the drug.

"What else can we give that will get us back in the game?" I asked her.

She said "We can try some calcium infusion. The blood we have given her has citrate in it and that chelates or binds the calcium the cells need to contract."

I asked "How much?"

She said "Let's try two amps."

I gave the orders.

I didn't expect anything dramatic until the second amp was running.

Half way through the second amp, the nurse said the bleeding was slowing down. Her blood pressure was holding without the dopamine support, and things were looking up.

Just a word of warning, Kathleen, whenever you bend over to smell the roses, something is looking to bite you in the ass. The nurse at the foot of the bed reported that the bleeding was increasing. One of the OB nurse practioners had been advising the other nurses and did an external exam and said that the uterus was not contracting.

The pharmacist heard the conversation, and took me aside. "We could try a prostaglandin drug, but the risk is uterine rupture, and maybe a sharp drop in blood pressure."

I said "The blood pressure we can manage with dopamine, we will have to chance the uterine problems otherwise we will lose her in the next hour or two. Have you got anything else?"

Curtly "No"

I asked "How long to get it from pharmacy?"

She said "Two seconds, it's already on the cart."

I said "Let's do it. Have I told you lately that I love you?"

She dropped her voice "Yeah, the last time you and I thrashed through one of these messes. By the way, that's a great song title."

She gave the drug to the nurse who gave it as an IM injection.

And we waited, watched the bleeding, the blood pressure, and the thin young woman in the bed.

The pharmacist had told me it would take about one half hour for anything to happen as the absorption from an IM injection is slow.

I went to get a cup of coffee, and checked on Sarah. Her vital signs were stable and she appeared to be awakening from the anesthesia. As I walked back to the other patient's room, her eyes followed me.

It was about twenty-five minutes after the injection that the nurse reported that the bleeding had stopped. Her pressure was stable, and the pupil continued to react to light.

The room looked like an abattoir. Blood was on the floor, spattered on the walls, blood soaked sheets were stuffed into the laundry hamper, and most of the nurses working at the end of the bed looked like ghouls.

But we had succeeded and could use the prostaglandin drug again if the bleeding resumed.

The next day, I asked one of my colleagues what he would have done in those circumstances. He said "Not that. You took a hell of a chance. What if she died? You used the rTPA in a post-op patient violating hospital protocol, against FDA recommendations. Mac, you can't count on luck all the time".

Sometimes it's better to be lucky than good. But he was right. It was a risk, for her and for me and the hospital staff who were involved. Beneficence, justice and non-malificence pushed to the limit if not beyond. But, you know why I went ahead? The girl in the bed could have been your sister.

I tried to recall when I had seen that much blood before. Neurology is usually a bloodless specialty. The only other time was more than thirty years ago in the Navy. I, as a general medical officer, was on an aircraft carrier that was carrying out training off the coast of California. Neophyte Marine pilots were practicing carrier landings in the A-4 Skyhawk, a relatively small but highly maneuverable attack aircraft compared to the larger F-4 and A-7 aircraft that the Navy pilots were flying. Landing on a carrier is probably the most difficult task for an aviator as he is trying to land on a moving target three hundred yards long, which is pitching and rolling at the same time. To make it a little easier, the carrier has a light system that shines a light beam three degrees vertically off the stern. If the pilot stays in the beam all the way to the deck, he will catch the second of four arresting wires, which is a perfect recovery. The pilot stays in the beam by adjusting power and the attitude or nose down angle of the aircraft. The pilot makes a down wind approach and then turns up wind to line up with the deck. From the up wind turn to recovery is only about fifteen seconds. The carrier is steaming into the wind but the pilot still has to keep up enough speed to get airborne if he misses the last wire. The moment the wheels touch the deck, the pilot goes to full power in case the tailhook misses the wire. If the pilot is too high or too low the landing signals officer will tell him to go around and try again, rather than risk colliding with the stern of the ship if he is too low or missing the last wire if he is too high and flying off the bow and falling into the ocean, either of which is fatal. All landings are recorded and discussed, and in a close knit group such as pilots, poor performance carries a price. Most of the experienced pilots had a light touch on stick and power, but the less experienced tend to overshoot and have to correct. If they are a tad too high and fast, rather than risk the jeers of their peers, they will cut power to get on the deck, resulting in a hard landing and possible aircraft damage.

Well, it was usually fun to watch the recoveries if you were off duty, and that's what two sailors were doing on a pleasant fall afternoon. They were up near the bow, sitting on some stowed wing tanks, which have fins on the tail end, and the sailors were straddling the tanks and the fins, watching the action. And then it happened. The pilot came in a little high and a little fast and did not get a wave off to go around again. He cut power and dumped it on the deck – hard. The front landing gear fractured and the wheel went down the deck at over one hundred miles an hour and smashed into the thigh of one of the sailors straddling the tanks. The fin amputated the leg, shattering the femur and slicing through the femoral artery. The whole thing took place in half a second. The sailor's screams over the noise of the jet engines alerted the corpsmen who were stationed on deck during air operations. One ran to the stricken man , pulled off his uniform web belt, took two wraps around the remaining thigh, threw a square knot in the belt, pulled a valve wrench off a nearby oxygen tank ,forced it into the belt and turned till the blood stop pumping onto the deck.

I had been on deck, standing by the island, and ran up the deck to see if I could help. The corpsman was holding the wrench, staring at the pool of blood, and the leg. I think he acted out of instinct and training and was too shocked to plan his next move. I told the second corpsman to get the stretcher and call for a transport team. The stricken sailor was unconscious due to shock, and we need to get him to sick bay and get blood donors ready. Once in sick bay, the surgeon tied off the artery and other small bleeders, and started direct transfusion from "volunteers" with his blood type. Eventually, he was loaded into the little turboprop transport, along with his leg, packed in ice and with a flight surgeon and catapulted off the deck to San Diego Naval Hospital two hundred miles over the horizon. The surgeons there made a valiant attempt to reattach his leg, but vascular surgical techniques were less developed then and he became an above knee amputee.

Anyway, there were two epilogues to the story of the lady with the postpartum stroke. The first is that she survived her lung disease and went to rehab where an MRI was done showing the remnants of a mid-brain stroke. The second is that her husband was a naval enlisted man and she was insured by virtue of his service. Unfortunately he had a trace of cannabis in his urine on a random drug test, so he was discharged from the service during her hospitalization and the government refused to pay any of her bills which were over several million dollars. I occasionally wonder if the drug test was fixed. In this business, no matter how cynical you get, you can't keep up.

All of us were drained. I went home; fed the dogs, let them have their time for fun and affection. I can't recall a time when I was not taking care of some living thing, chickens, lab animals, pets, kids, spouse, and patients. Now, all that was left were the dogs and the patients.

I thought back, while I was trying to go to sleep, how variable has been my experience with the drug. The last young woman I treated with rTPA was one of our nurses, a woman about fifty or so who was brought to the emergency room after having the onset of a right sided weakness, and difficulty talking about an hour before I saw her in the ED. She had had a history of a cardiac arrhythmia, that later turned out to be atrial fibrillation. Her CT was negative for any hemorrhage and I treated her according to the hospital thrombolytic protocol, which says no aspirin or anticoagulants can be given for twenty-four hours after the thrombolytic infusion. The infusion seemed to work and in an hour she was moving her right side and speaking. She was admitted to ICU and was stable for the first six hours. I checked on her before I went home and was still satisfied that all was well. The next morning, a repeat CT scan showed a small stroke, but no bleeding and her clotting studies were coming back to normal. An ultrasound study showed occlusion of a major cerebral artery on the left, consistent with her right-sided symptoms. She had enough blood flow from the right side vessels to preserve her left hemisphere.

Because she was at risk for further embolization from her cardiac arrhythmia, I ordered a heparin drip to be started twenty-four hours after the TPA infusion had been completed. The hospital has a protocol to adjust the dose to the patient's weight and that was what I ordered. The infusion started at six PM and at midnight, the nurses called to say that she had a headache and was not as responsive. I ordered an immediate CT scan and dressed and headed in to the hospital, dreading the result.

The CT scan showed a massive hemorrhage beginning in the area of the stroke and spreading into the ventricle, and shifting the hemisphere five millimeters to the right. I called the neurosurgeons, and ordered six units of fresh frozen plasma to replace her clotting factors, but I knew the cause was lost, probably when the heparin drip began. The neurosurgeons did not want to operate as the only thing they could do was take out the dead brain and blood clot, but the likelihood of survival was miniscule and if she survived, she still would be paralyzed and unable to speak or understand. I spoke with her husband, as did the neurosurgeons and the decision was to do nothing and keep her comfortable.

Then the vigil began. I ordered as needed narcotics, to alleviate any visible discomfort, but that was mostly for the bystanders. Since she had worked at the hospital quite awhile and was well known in the community, all her friends came to the bedside, as did the CEO of the hospital, all the doctors she worked with in the operating rooms, the director of nursing , and her children, church members and for all I knew the governor and state assembly members.

Twelve hours, then twenty- four, then thirty- six, the watch was kept. I knew they needed time, not just to say goodbye, because that doesn't take much time. No, they needed time to love again in a way they never would again.

Finally, her closest friend in the operating room, a woman I had known for several years, came to me and said "End it, they can't take any more." So I did.

Lawyers visit their failures, architects cover theirs with ivy. Doctors bury their failures along with a piece of themselves.

CHAPTER 7

The next day, the nephrologists started the plasmaphoresis procedure, hooking Sarah's vascular access catheters to a machine the size of a bookcase. The machine is basically a continuous flow centrifuge that takes blood from one of the catheters, separates the plasma from the cells, remixes the cells with an artificial plasma mixture, and reinfuses the solution. This removes all the proteins, including the antibody proteins believed to be attacking the nerve-muscle junction. Sessions take hours and the process is repeated on alternate days to let the body recover. Hopefully the process removes the bad antibody faster than the body can make it.

I stopped by Sarah's bed on my rounds as the plasmaphoresis was underway. She was sleeping but woke when I entered the room. I got a half smile and a view of gray eyes under half closed lids. I sat down next to the bed and she reached for my hand. I held her hand and just looked at her for a minute or so not really conscious of the technician tending his equipment. Since she could not speak, I would have to frame my questions so a binary reply could be made.

"Are you in pain?" Brief shake
"Do you feel any stronger?" Brief nod.

"Much stronger?" Brief shake

"A little?" Nod.

"Squeeze my fingers." A very definite increase of pressure and then a relaxation, but she did not let go.

"Open your eyes and smile." Very briefly, the eyes opened and a smile fled across her face.

"That's beautiful and so are you" Another brief smile and a slight increase in pressure on my hand.

I said "This process will take about ten days to complete, and maybe at the end, we can get you off the ventilator. I'll keep the steroids and the other medications going in the meantime. I'll check on you several times a day. Once you're better, you will have to take medications for years but should be able to live a normal life." I wanted to ask her if there was anything she needed or wanted, but realized that anything beyond a gesture or scribbled note was beyond her power. I made up my mind to ask the speech pathologists to set up a communication system that would give her some sense of control. In the meantime, gestures and a touch would have to do. I stood up to leave but she held on to my hand briefly, and then let go and closed her eyes. For both of us waiting was all there was.

Waiting is one of the hidden aspects of medicine, waiting for lab results, X-ray reports, drugs to work, waiting. Doctors are not known for patience. Rather than wait, we rush off to do something else, see another patient, and write chart notes, anything than wait. This is maybe the reason why we jump into a therapy or a drug regimen before we know what is really going on. The external pressures from insurance companies and hospital administrators to get people out of the hospital as fast as possible contribute to our impatience. Waiting takes peace of mind, a rare quality.

Walking back to the nursing station, I was aware that I had a feeling I had met her some other time but the circumstances eluded me. I was also aware that I felt a sense of affection for her, something

I had not felt for another person for some time. This was not pity or empathy but something other, and was possibly a problem ethically. I knew I needed to know more about her as a person, not as a patient. Her family was visiting on a daily basis, and I asked the nurses to let me know when they were in the hospital so I could talk to them. Back at the office, I passed her name and date of birth to the records clerk, but her search turned up nothing. Still the feeling was there that I had met her somewhere.

The next day, her son and daughter were in the ICU conference room for an update on their mother's condition. Her daughter was a college senior, petite, blonde and somewhat shy. Her son was older, perhaps twenty-two, and seemed to be a mechanic, judging from his hand and clothes. Her name was Susan and he was Jack. I told them about the plasmaphoresis treatment and how long it would take and the possible treatments to follow. I filled them in on the lab data that was available and what it meant. After all their questions had been answered, I said "I have a vague feeling that I've seen your mother before but not as a patient and not socially."

Her daughter answered "She was never a patient of yours but you did take care of her mother about ten years ago. Grandma had a stroke and you were the neurologist that managed her care. Mom was impressed with how hard you worked to save her."

I asked "What was the patient's name?"
She replied "She was Cecilia Daugherty"

Some of the details came back to me. I'm better at remembering cases than remembering names. She was a late middle aged lady with a massive left hemisphere stroke that developed a lot of cerebral edema in the stroke site and began to develop brain herniation, which is when the swollen tissue compresses the rest of the normal brain and cuts off blood flow to the normal side. I tried osmotic agents and forced hyperventilation to try to shrink the dead tissue but these maneuvers quickly lost effectiveness. I asked the neurosurgeons to decompress the brain by removing the skull on one side and removing the dead brain .Citing literature at the time, they refused on the grounds that the procedure was futile. . She died in a few days, and other than those details of the case, I could not recall any other memories of the incident.

I asked the daughter, "Tell me about your mother"
She asked "What do you need to know?"
I said "Well, I'd like to know what work she does, how much education she has, what social support she has."

She thought for a moment and said "Well, she is the director of nutrition at a resort; she is a registered dietician who used to work here at the hospital. She had one year of med school, but had to quit."
I was curious and asked "What happened? Usually once a person is accepted to med school, they finish."
She sighed, "It's a long story. She and my dad married while both were in college. He is an accountant and runs his own firm. Her older sister went to med school and then into research and now is head of a large biotech company. Her father was a pharmacist, so there was a lot of pressure to do medicine. You know what med school is like. You have no life and she had two babies. My Dad felt neglected and had a problem with anger. They divorced, she got the house and us and a brief hospitalization for depression. Once she got better, with some help from her dad she went back for her Masters degree in nutrition and the dietician certificate. She got the job at the hospital, and raised us, paid the mortgage, kept her old Honda wagon running until the resort hired her at twice the pay of this place."

I asked "How come she did not remarry?"
She replied "I don't know except that she was raised Catholic and still goes to Mass and Communion. Also, most single men of her age are single for a reason, and most don't want to be burdened with two little kids."

I asked "What contact does your dad keep with her and you?"

She said "He pays for some of my brother's and my expenses but they don't talk much."

I asked, "What about her family?"

She said "She visits her sister once in a while, her Dad is still in pretty good health, and she has a brother in San Francisco that she sees about twice a year. She has some friends from her church and Bible study, but she doesn't go out much."

I said, "Thank you for the information. I'm not sure what I'll do with it but I feel better knowing more about her."

She paused and then said, "Doctor, my mother trusts you a lot."

I said, "I offered her the option to get another neurologist, but she refused. Anytime you or she decides that you want someone else, I'll arrange it. Until then, I'll take care of her as long as she needs or until she decides otherwise. I may want to get a second opinion in any case just to be sure that every base has been covered."

We left it at that. I would have a better idea of what help I would need as the plasmaphoresis progressed.

I went to Sarah's bedside after talking with her family, and sat down with her chart. I made a note that I had discussed her progress with her family. As I wrote I noticed that she was watching me. I looked up and said "I hadn't realized that we had met before. Your kids told me that I took care of your mother some time ago."

She nodded.

I continued "I also asked them about your personal history, jobs, marriage, that sort of thing. I guess I wanted to know more about you, but I think now that I should not have asked. I was invading your privacy. I apologize"

She shook her head.

Puzzled, I asked "No? Do you mean "no" I should not apologize?'

Nod.

I said, "Well, I probably was prying. I didn't realize what a bad time you had had back then. You made a successful career and raised two children single-handed. The kids seem to be well adjusted and mature. Is your ex involved with them?"

Shake

I said "They also told me that you worked here for some time after school. I'm sure we must have passed in the hall many times"

Nod and smile.

I added "Your kids told me you're Catholic."

Nod

I asked "Would you like the Catholic chaplain to visit?"

Nod

I said "I will ask him to come by tomorrow. Is there anything else I can do for you now?"

She reached for her writing pad and pencil and wrote "I'm scared. I'd like you to stay with me as much as you can."

I said "Alright."

She wrote "Promise?'

I replied "Promise."

She dropped the pencil and tore off the top sheet of the writing pad and pushed it toward me. When I reached to take it she took my hand and briefly interlaced her fingers with mine and then let go and lay back and closed her eyes. I put the paper in my pocket and took the chart back to the nursing station.

When I made rounds the next day, she seemed stronger and her breathing test showed a slight improvement. The head of the bed was elevated and the foot of the bed was lowered so it was as if she was in a recliner chair. Her head was supported by bolsters on each side. She was having a plasmaphoresis treatment on my morning walk by and I stopped briefly at her bedside. The nurses had brushed her hair and applied some lipstick and powder. She looked cheerful but somewhat pale despite the cosmetics. Plasmaphoresis removes a good many things from the blood in addition to the antibodies causing her disease. One of the things removed is a hormone that stimulates the bone marrow, so that after a few treatments, patients develop a mild anemia. I made a note to self to check her blood count after the series was complete.

I noted on the chart cover that the chaplain had been by and administered the Last Rites. The term Last Rites sound so final, even though the Church encourages the administration whenever a Catholic is seriously ill. I sat down by the bed opposite the plasmaphoresis equipment. The tech was making adjustments and changing IV bags and paying no attention to us. In addition to the pad of paper and a pencil, the speech therapists had provided her with a small whiteboard on a stand and a marker which looked easier for her to use.

I said "I see the chaplain has been by. Was that OK?"

She wrote "Yes, thanks."

I said "I hope you didn't misinterpret the Last Rites as an end, if you know what I mean."

She wrote "No, comfort. Sacrament of Sick now."

I replied "I stand corrected. I haven't kept up with the terminology."

"Are you Catholic?" she asked.

"Sometimes" I replied

"Meaning?" she wrote.

I don't usually discuss my religion or lack of it with patients so I was stuck for an answer. Probably the best thing would have been to avoid any discussion of religion or spirituality, because it goes to the heart of being. And every person's journey is unique.

But I didn't blow her off. I suppose that if I had done so, the final result would have been the same, save for the pain.

I said "I think sometimes that it's all true, that God is and His promise is forever, and then I think, maybe that we are just complex chemistry and the third law of thermodynamics rules, and when we die there is nothing left of us."

She wrote, "How do you live?"

It took me a moment to think. I said, "I guess like a lot of people, from day to day, responding to the needs of the moment, with a bit of faith and a bit of doubt hand in hand, and no promise of resolution one way or the other."

She wrote "Pascal"

I knew what she meant. Pascal's wager, that with eternity in the balance, one should act as if God was.

I said "Pascal was a mathematician and therefore logical. I don't think faith is a matter of logic. Maybe a gift, maybe a need, but I could not reason to belief. Besides, in this town, the house always wins."

She wrote "Cradle Catholic?'

"Yeah, the whole bit." I replied

She wrote "Altar boy?" and had a slight smile on her face.

I said "Once upon a time. Maybe not much left of that person"

She wrote "Gone or hidden?"

It was my turn to smile "The altar boy's job was to respond for the people in the church in the old Latin Mass. We memorized the Latin responses. It was like a long running play, say your lines and move on. The altar boy's responses were found wanting."

She wrote "Wanting what?"

I replied "Answers"

She put the marker down and lay back, and looked away from me at the other enclosed beds.

She looked back, took up the marker and wrote "For them, you or me?"

Just like a board exam- multiple choice-maybe all the above

My reply "Answers about how to keep going when there are no answers."

She wrote "No answers or none you like?"

She had me there.

It never fails to amaze me how fast a conversation in a hospital can penetrate to the bone, almost as though the scrubs and hospital gowns leave us naked.

I wanted to ask her if she had had doubts, but I could see that she was tiring as the plasmaphoresis proceeded. Anyway, I wanted to change the subject for now, so I asked her "Do you have a regular pastor or parish visitor?"

She wrote "St. John's"

I said "All right, I'll have the social worker notify the parish that you're here"

She nodded and reached for my hand, interlaced her fingers with mine and then laid back and closed her eyes.

CHAPTER 8

Thursday was nearly a week since Sarah was admitted. It was my on call night for the city. Most of the times when I'm on call for the ED, I see new patients, rarely people I've seen before. After my conversation with Sarah, the evening began with a couple of minor problems, most of which were solved by talking to the ED physician. Then about nine PM, a city hospital ED called about one of my former patients. I had cared for her about three years before for a brain hemorrhage which left her with a left sided weakness. Since then her elderly husband had cared for her, taking her to therapy in a van equipped for a wheelchair. The wheelchair was usually locked in place in the center of the van, just beside and a little back of the driver, and just behind the extension of the engine compartment. The old couple was on the freeway when a car slowed or stopped suddenly in front of them. The driver stamped on the power brake, and the old lady flew forward and face planted on the engine compartment housing, as she had not been belted into the wheelchair.

The paramedics extricated her from the car and intubated her in the field prior to transport. In the ED the CT scan showed a lot of blood, both a subdural hemorrhage, which is blood between the bone and the brain, and a subarachnoid hemorrhage, blood all over the surface of the brain and extending down into the brain tissue. The ED physician called me and the on call neurosurgeon, who was a newcomer to the neurosurgical group, which was the only neurosurgical group in the area. He was Irish, volatile and occasionally vulgar and very well trained. Also ambitious, which seemingly put him at odds with the more senior neurosurgeons.

We both examined her and agreed that the blunt force trauma was devastating and the small subdural hematoma was not in need of evacuation. Both of us reviewed her living will which was on file in her hospital record and her desire in such a situation was for comfort care. Her husband agreed. But before we moved her to the ICU her pastor arrived, notified by the hospital. He was an elderly priest that I recognized from the church that I attended when the mood struck. He anointed her with the Sacrament of the Sick, prayed with her husband and departed for his rectory about midnight. She departed for the ICU.

The next morning, I walked into the old ICU to her bedside. I first noted that she was triggering the ventilator, and had some spontaneous movement of her right side. Looking more closely, I saw that she had normal size and reactive pupils. I thought for a moment-did that old priest pull off a miracle with his blessed oil and prayers? Regardless, he gave us a problem. Since she had improved, we would have to support her rather than taking her off the ventilator. The neurosurgeon followed me in and we both then went to X-Ray to look at the morning's head CT scan. The subarachnoid blood was the same, and the subdural was no larger. Still, we both agreed there was no need for surgery. Also, I wanted to keep her in ICU for a while, at least till she was extubated and able to protect her airway.

The neurosurgeon was leaving town to attend a meeting, and I assumed one of his associates or nurses would follow the patient's course. His professional relations were only part of this story. The other major part was the hospital, which, I forgot to mention was Catholic. Well, not much happened to her for about two days. Then just before six AM, the ICU nurse called to report that she was less alert and her pupils were unequal. I ordered an immediate CT scan and threw on some jeans and a sweat shirt and drove to the hospital and went immediately to X-ray. The subdural hematoma that we assumed was minor had massively enlarged, compressing the brain under it and worse, had compressed the brain stem. After giving orders for an osmotic agent to shrink the brain and buy some time, I called the neurosurgeon on call, only to get the one senior surgeon the Irishman was having difficulties with. I had to put up with a few minutes of listening to his raging about his colleague abandoning this patient and had to remind him that this was an emergency and failure to respond would result in a call to the chief of the medical staff. He finally agreed to take her to surgery for burr hole drainage of the hematoma, muttering that it was a futile gesture. Well, he was right on one thing, it was futile, and she did not awaken.

Now we were back to square one- irreversible coma. Her living will was still in effect, so the appropriate thing to do was to extubate her and then see if she would breathe on her own. I had guessed that she would, because the hematoma had not completely damaged the lower brainstem where the centers for respiration and blood pressure control were located. The next step in carrying out her wishes would be to stop the IV fluids. This is where we or I have a bit of a problem. The hospital and the Catholic Church have strong moral objections to depriving the comatose of hydration. They feel that the value of human life does not rest on awareness or sentience. The hospital sometimes solves the problem by transferring the patient to a non-religiously affiliated nursing home.

However, this family was embedded in the Church and wanted her to stay in the hospital and die there. Her living will overrode the hospital's moral qualms and was preeminent by state law. I have never been comfortable with just cutting off the fluids. Oh, I know the literature says that there is not great discomfort, and that death occurs in about six days more or less. Still, no one has come back to say "Well, that wasn't all that bad." So I like to run a drip of opiate and tranquilizer, not enough to depress respiration, but enough to wipe away anxiety and pain.

So I wrote my usual orders for hyrdomorphone and lorazepam and checked on the patient daily. On the third day, she looked good, too good, good skin turgor, no smell of uremia. Since she was on comfort care the usual input –output records were not kept. Looking back through the medication administration record, I note she was getting close to sixty ccs per hour of fluids, not much below the seventy-five cc's per hour that will sustain a normal person for weeks.

Now it was my turn to rage at this subtle sabotage. I tracked down the nurse and the pharmacist and explained as clearly as I could that they could get the drugs into a form so that she would get only ten cc's per hour. After a bit of grumbling they agreed. The hospital had put her in a large private room, almost a suite, with a view of the western mountains which was spectacular at sunset. Her husband and daughter stayed there most of the day. He was stricken with guilt and anticipatory grief but firm in his decision not to continue support. I visited with them daily, often twice daily, in part to be sure she was not in distress, and partly just to chat. She died peacefully about five days after I changed the fluid orders. The family seemed OK and when I ran into the husband at church, he thanked me for her care and invited me to go fishing at his place on the lake. I never did go as he died two months later. The nurses didn't speak to me for a month.

The outcome of the Irishmen's story is that the neurosurgical group, led by the senior surgeon expelled him from the group, using his management of this case as the excuse. Apparently they thought he would pack up and leave town. Not so, he formed his own group and the natural monopoly that neurosurgery had enjoyed, that enabled them to control their fate with regard to hospitals and insurance carriers was gone for good. Such is the medical ego.

During this period, my conversation with Sarah continued. Friday, the day after the old lady was admitted; I checked Sarah's respiratory function data which looked better. She was starting to accumulate some fluid due to the steroids, noticeable as a slight fullness to her face. I made a note to follow her blood glucose levels, and sat down at her bedside. This was an off day for plasmaphoresis, and she appeared more rested.

She seemed stronger and was able to keep her eyes open more. Her smile was a treat. She wrote "Good morning sunshine" on her whiteboard. "Still looking for answers?" was the second line.

It seemed like a good time to ask her about her past, especially the struggles her kids had mentioned.

I said "Always, how about some help? How did you get through the bad time after your divorce?"

She seemed to think for a minute, and then wrote "Counseling, drugs, Family. And prayer".

I asked "Did you ever doubt your faith?"

Nod. "Years"

I asked, "What caused the break?"

She wrote "Did everything right, church, school, marriage, and failed."

I asked, "Did you go away mad or just go away?"

She wrote "Drifted, tried other churches. Not the same, not home."

I asked "You must have thought about remarriage? You were young, attractive, employed."

Nod

She wrote "Boyfriend, not Catholic. Didn't understand"

"Didn't understand what?" I asked.

"No remarriage" she wrote.

"Now I don't understand." I said. "You left the Church but still followed the rules?"

Nod

"That's a little nuts, don't you think?" I asked.

Nod. Small smile.

"How about the prayers?" I asked.

"Couldn't" She wrote.

I asked "Who then?"

She wrote "Parents, friends."

"When did you go back?" I asked.

She wrote "Good Friday ten years ago. What about you?"

I said "Sixteen years of Catholic education and I learned a lot about the Faith but not a lot about faith. What little faith there was comes and goes."

She wrote "And now?"

I thought for a moment and said, "Just an old man whose children are grown and gone. I live alone except for two dogs. But I think you were asking about my belief. I call myself Catholic, because that's the culture that I know. But, there are only a few things in the belief that move me. I guess the Eucharist is the main thing. But sometimes I'm totally without any spiritual feeling at all and can only let the music wash over me to find any peace. I had a dream once that still troubles me, I was driving fast along a road bordering a cliff and missed a turn and went over the cliff. I expected to die in the impact, but when it came, there was nothing but silence, a silence such as I have only experienced in the wilderness. I thought, this is what death is, utter silence, nothingness. Only later did I think, how was I aware of the silence, what did that mean, was that hell or heaven?"

She wrote "No God or Light?"

I said, "No, but it was a dream and probably means nothing."

She wrote "Sorry" Then "I wish you had my faith".

I said "What is is. My wife was a life-long Southern Protestant and we discussed religion for thirty years and that accomplished nothing but to drive us apart. I finally gave it up and went my way religiously, which wasn't very far.

She wrote "Thanks" and laid down her marker and took my hand once again.

CHAPTER 9

I later reviewed her pulmonary function data with the pulmonary specialists. We were getting close to the end of the plasmaphoresis series and their opinion was that she still was not strong enough to support her own respiration. I knew I would have to bring up the need for tracheostomy and probably placement of a feeding tube into the stomach. It was puzzling that after three treatments she had only improved about fifty percent in inspiratory strength. Ordinarily, I would have expected more improvement. But there were two more treatments in this series, and I hoped to put off a decision for a week. Besides, the lab studies for myasthenia and its variants were still not back in the chart.

I finished my rounds and went to the office. I had an hour before the scheduled appointments, and had planned to review some medical records for an upcoming court case in which I was listed as an expert witness. Sarah's probing of my beliefs or lack of same was still on my mind. She seemed to be as concerned for my spiritual state as I was for her physical state. I often envy those older people in my practice who seem to be settled in their faith, whatever it is, because I think they got that certainty through their life struggles. I'm old and all I got is doubt.

I try not to discuss religion with patients, mostly because it's not my job. Also, I think doubt can be infectious. And it's not my job to hinder faith.

Still, her intensity was contagious. I put the file aside for a moment to reflect on the conversation. Whose position is valid or logical? Her faith now reflected mine of years gone by. Yet she had left that faith because she had failed at life as she and the Church had expected it to be. Had the faith failed her or did she fail the faith? I can't imagine trying to do med school with two babies and a needy husband. Only a super woman would attempt it, or someone who thought she was superwoman. The valproic acid as her only prescribed medication would make sense if she was hypomanic. Absent a seizure disorder, its only other common use is for bipolar disorder. Did her biochemistry push her into a situation where failure was inevitable? I knew I would need to ask her but I might not fully understand.

There is a huge gap in our knowledge of neurobiology. We know in a rough sort of way how nerve cells talk to one another using chemicals that open pores in the membrane that then generates an electrical impulse. The electrical impulse travels down a nerve fiber to another nerve cell, where it releases another chemical. We also know, in a general way, that some groups of cells are linked to others. And we know that certain brain regions have specialized functions. What we don't know is how the neurochemistry, neurophysiology and neuroanantomy yield thought and reasoning. How does neurochemistry come to know chemistry let alone conceive of God? There is another thing, the process of thinking changes the brain doing the thinking. The uncertainty principle seems not limited to sub-atomic physics. Somehow we wound up with a brain more sophisticated than we need for mere survival and reproduction which is the only criterion that evolution cares about.

Her marriage and faith ended in a cataclysmic event. There is an axiom in medicine that acute events get better quickly- or not at all. How had I ventured away? My life was more like chronic disease, a slow slide, and possibly more irreversible for all that. Still, there is always the possibility of redemption in this land of second chances.

This was leading nowhere. I picked up the file and began a quick review to establish the facts, what happened, who knew what and when. Was the outcome the result of untreatable disease or was there medical error and if there was, was it pertinent.

The case involved an older woman who died of a subarachnoid hemorrhage. The diagnosis was missed until the patient was transferred to St. James due to deteriorating condition. At that point an MRI showed traces of the blood and extensive stroke due to vasospasm, a not uncommon complication of such hemorrhage. About twenty-five percent of patients with subarachnoid will die on the spot, mostly due to cardiac arrhythmia induced by the bleed. Later deaths are due to repeat bleeding or spasm of the arteries due to breakdown products of the old blood. The death rate has not changed much in the last fifty years.

She had been brought to the other emergency department complaining of a sudden severe headache, and decreased alertness. The emergency department physician who examined her did not record any abnormal findings and ordered a CT scan with intravenous contrast. The hospital radiologist reported this study as normal. The patient was admitted to the hospital, given pain medication, and after two days was unresponsive. I could see a couple of problems at the first read through. Why was a non-contrast scan not done first? If it was done why was there no report? The non-contrast scan would have shown the blood with a seventy to ninety percent probability. Why was no lumbar puncture done? Even with a negative CT scan, the LP would have picked up traces of bleeding or detected signs of infection to explain the patient's symptoms. And there was the question of why was she allowed to deteriorate without further studies? That part was easy, she was the wife of a prominent physician and no one wanted to disturb her. If I ever get dragged into the hospital, I hope I'm wearing dirty jeans, a two-day growth of beard and no deodorant and no ID. That way they will pay attention to my illness and not my profession.

I would need to read the record again before I talked to the attorney, which would involve giving him a quick course in CT scans and subarachnoid hemorrhage. I would probably have to go to the outside hospital and rummage through their X-Ray file room to see if the non-contrast scan ever existed. And I mean talk, as at this stage, the attorneys want nothing in writing that would be subject to discovery.

I went through the office work with half a mind, listening, advising, writing prescriptions and ordering studies, all the while rolling around in my mind what to do if Sarah did not turn around with the steroids and plasmaphoresis. A lot would depend on the outstanding lab studies. I would eventually need to get her off the high dose steroids, before she developed diabetes and osteoporosis. The alternatives were not attractive as most were cancer chemotherapeutic agents that provoke bone marrow failure and reduce resistance to infection. An additional option would be to get another opinion from one of my colleagues.

But who?

It occurred to me to wonder why I was so obsessive about this case. Obsessive compulsive traits are common in doctors and may make for success if not happiness. Still this was over the top even for me. I'm a little beyond the stage where`a woman's sexuality can divert me from focusing on the medical aspect of a case. So it had to something within my personality at work. I have woman friends at work that I care about and who care about me, but I don't relate to them as I did to Sarah. She had gotten beyond her situation and reached out to me with a perception of my uncertainty and vulnerability. And I don't think she did it to distract herself. On the other hand, there is an issue of dependency. Patients are powerless and afraid which can make them attempt to win the doctor's favor.

Their vulnerability introduces a relative imbalance in power that can cloud a professional's judgment. I realized that I should discuss the problem with somebody, but I was afraid that the advice would be to sign off the case but that would be the patient's decision and besides, I didn't want the relationship to end.

The hospital has a separate lunch room for doctors, as most work over the lunch period. The place is small, noisy, and crowded with staff doctors, residents and med students. There is a big screen TV running either sports or an all news channel. Not much of a place to get advice, but it was a rare week that some doctor didn't ask my opinion about a patient. I managed to secure a place next to the hospital's liaison psychiatrist, Dr. James Marlowe, and waited till others had left. He worked for the university and had trained at a large city hospital in the South. He shaved his head, wore a fedora, and often dressed like a Chicago gangster. And unlike most psychiatrists of my acquaintance, his approach to issues was direct if not blunt.

I asked "Can I run something by you?"

Moderately pained expression "Sure".

I asked "What would you advise a physician that developed a friendship with a patient?"

He kept his voice down which made his Southern accent more noticeable "We're talking you here, right?'

I replied, "Yeah, I'm the one."

Bluntly he asked "Is this sexual? A current or future lover or mistress? I presume this person is a she."

I replied "Yes to the second, no to the first."

"Has this woman been a friend before she became ill" He asked.

"No."

He paused, "You know why we don't take care of friends or family, our judgment becomes faulty, our love gets in the way of thinking. So get off the case, for your sake and hers."

I replied "I already suggested that and she refused."

He said "Then get another neurologist in for a second opinion, preferable one of your older colleagues if there are any. And have him follow the case with you, not just write an opinion and leave"

"Thanks, I'll do that. I think Weston is still in town though he is partially retired." As I got up to leave, he put his hand on my arm and said "One other thought. This is something that ain't over when it's over. Given your age and personal situation, this could be a personal and professional disaster. It's possible to practice without much personal involvement. In fact it's better that way. Caring makes you vulnerable and sometimes the more you care, the more you lose."

It was good advice. I knew he would not raise the issue again until I did.

I had some consults to see, one of which was in the ICU. The first was a young woman, who began to have convulsive seizures that could not be controlled in the ED and was now on the respirator, paralyzed with a curare- like drug, and on a midazolam drip. The EEG showed that the seizures had stopped, but she had sustained cardiac damage. The urine drug screen was not back yet but a brief inspection of her mouth suggested methamphetamine use. For reasons that still escape me, methamphetamine users have terrible dentition, what the ED docs call meth mouth. Her CT scan showed a lot of brain swelling. The EEG was showing very slow activity, but she was on a very high dose of sedative. The cardiac changes could be due to the seizures or due to the methamphetamine. Her liver and kidney function were great. She was not pregnant. If the cardiac changes reversed, she might be a donor candidate, assuming of course that she did not have AIDS or hepatitis. The middle-aged nurse from the regional transplant network was hovering in the background. I had no idea if there was family available, or whether she had designated herself as a donor on her driver's license.

There are two ways to be dead. You're dead if you heart stops permanently. The other way is for your brain to die or cease to function permanently. The death of the rest of the body follows but not immediately. The concept of brain death was defined some twenty years ago and incorporated into state laws. The statutes basically say that there has to be death of the whole brain and neurologic practice parameters make this into a test of brainstem function with ancillary tests to determine brain cortex function. This is a hard test to meet. And the procedures to preserve organs in a potential donor often damage the brain. The ethical principle is that organs cannot be harvested from living people when that process would result in death. Since there are more potential recipients than donors, there is a lot of pressure to identify potential donors early in their hospital course .A patient with a dead or dying brain is considered a potential beating heart donor. One beating heart donor may contribute two kidneys, a liver, pancreas, heart, lungs, corneas, skin and bone. The scarcity can be a temptation to be less than rigorous in determining brain death. There have been rumors of sales of organs harvested from executed prisoners in China. Of course, a bullet in the back of the head makes for a fairly definite brain death. Most English-speaking countries prohibit payment to donors, but other counties, such as Iran do permit kidney donors to be paid, often quite a lot. The ethics of this are mixed. Autonomy would suggest that your body is yours to dispose of, since you can survive pretty well with one kidney, with luck. Still, there is an element of coercion in offering a large sum of money to a poor man whose family is starving.

Neurologists get involved with the determination of brain death and its cause and wind up mediating the donation process as a neutral party. I was still a long way from that with this young lady. I would first have to get her off the sedatives and paralytics to make any determination. Given that she had some brain activity on EEG, the final event would be cerebral edema causing herniation of the brain into the foramen magnum at the base of the skull where the spinal cord begins.

I spoke to the transplant network nurse, and let her know it would be a few days before any determination could be made. She had already started the preliminary testing on the basis of the declaration on the patient's driver's license. Even if family turned up, that declaration was binding.

Sarah was two rooms down, and probably heard my voice. She was on her fourth plasmaphoresis treatment, and was pale. Her blood pressure on the monitor seemed low and I mentioned this to the technician. He said he would fix it with the artificial plasma infusion. I looked at settings on the ventilator, and it seemed that they were reducing the support somewhat. She gave me a weak smile and picked up the white board and marker and wrote "Talk?"

"Sure" I said.

She wrote "How much better?"

I replied "50%"

She wrote "Enough?"

"No" I said.

"Then?" She wrote.

I said "Finish this series and see if a second series is needed."

She pointed to the ET tube, then wrote "And?"

I said "I'll probably have to have a tracheostomy done and have a feeding tube placed, a PEG tube."

She wrote "When?"

I said "Early next week."

"OK" She wrote.

I waited a moment and said "I want to ask another neurologist for a second opinion.'

She looked at me for a moment then quickly wrote "OK but promise me you won't quit- no matter what- no matter what."

When she wrote that she looked at me for a longer moment and I saw a tear form.

I said "OK, I promise."

She leaned back and closed her eyes as if the emotional effort had exhausted her.

She opened her eyes, took my hand and gave it a soft squeeze. Then she picked up the white board and wrote "Tell me more about you."

"What's to know?" I asked.

She wrote "What do you do for fun? Read?"

"I read some history, an occasional novel, some poetry, and the Bible occasionally."

She smiled weakly and wrote "Bible? Still looking?"

"I find the Psalms helpful at times." I said.

"Which?" she wrote.

I said, "130"

She wrote "Out of the depths. Felt like that once.'

I asked "Before you came back?"

She wrote "On my way-still"

I asked "Still?"

She nodded.

I said "I thought once back, you stayed."

She wrote "Journey, with detours"

She was clearly tiring, so I said "I'll see you later."

She motioned me to come closer, and as I did and went to brush the hair back from her face, she took my hand and touched it to her lips and then lay back

Chapter 10

The last words she wrote were still with me as I walked back to my office. Her faith journey had a direction despite detours. Mine was more like wandering. Of course there is the bumper sticker that reads "Not all who wander are lost." Either way, we would walk together for a time. Unless the treatments were effective, her journey would end in Emmaus. I knew for certain that I would need to get hold of Weston.

He had had a long career as an academic neurologist at a large Western university. On his retirement from that position, he moved to our area and taught at our little medical school. He was an artist, an athlete, and lived high up in the mountains. In spring, summer and fall, he rode a bike all over town from hospital to hospital and to the university. In winter, he lived to cross country ski. He seldom wore a tie and looked like a mountain man from frontier days. He despised lawyers and they hated to have to consult him as an expert as he was brusque almost to the point of rudeness. In addition, as his handwriting was illegible, they always had to ask him to translate. He retired after the only malpractice ever filed against him was adjudicated in his favor. Since I was the principal expert witness for the defense, I hoped he would be willing to help. I called his home between patient visits. His wife answered and said he was on a backpacking trip and would be back in a few days. She would ask him to call back but made no commitments.

I was on call that evening, and hoped that the caseload would be light. Before I went home, I reviewed Sarah's most recent lab data. Her respiratory function studies were now sixty percent of normal, still not enough to allow her to be off all respiratory support for a prolonged period. The speech pathologists had put off a swallowing evaluation till she was extubated. Her blood sugar was a bit high, probably due to the anti-inflammatory steroids. None of this was unexpected. What were unexpected were the results of the antibody tests for myasthenia gravis. Neither the blocking nor the binding antibody could be detected in her blood.

As you now know Kathleen, there is a myasthenic-like syndrome caused by an antibody that blocks the release of acetylcholine from the nerve side of the neuromuscular junction. This antibody is often associated with certain lung cancers, which I was fairly sure the Sarah did not have on the basis of her chest CT scan. Nevertheless, the Lambert-Eaton syndrome or myasthenic syndrome often looks like myasthenia gravis in that the eye and throat muscles are affected. It even transiently responds to the acetyl cholinesterase inhibiting drugs used to treat the garden variety myasthenia gravis. The antibody test for Lambert-Eaton syndrome was still outstanding and clearly, this was an area that Weston would have to address.

Sarah appeared to be sleeping and I did not disturb her because the plasmaphoresis was stressful for her. There was another reason. Despite my growing fondness for her and my pleasure in her company, her perceptive questions were challenging my vague rational skepticism.

You see, the Church I grew up in was very different from the one you were baptized in thirty-five years later. It was different still from the Church that Sarah knew. Vatican II happened and everything seemed to change. The priest turned around in more than one way and the Latin was gone. The Church of my childhood and young adulthood was one of rules and ritual and faith was assumed. Catholic grade school, Catholic high school and college were a continuous culture of shared experience and intellectual structure. This happy state of mind did not collapse immediately, but eroded with experience and time.

You know we moved a lot when you were young. Most physicians, when they finish their training, find a congenial area to live and practice and stay there most of their lives. They become part of the community and its institutions. Not us, we moved a lot and I'm sure you knew only part of the reason. My fledgling academic career ended when the incoming departmental chairman wanted salary lines for his people. So we moved. New job at a private institute that lasted several years until the chairman and managing partner used partnership money to buy and install multi-million dollar imaging equipment in defiance of state regulation. When some partners, including myself, objected, he dissolved the partnership. So we moved. Short time in the Southwest in private practice that ended when I defended a physician in a peer review meeting. The meeting had been convened by the hospital against one of their radiologists. He had noted that angiographic procedures were taking three times longer than normal because the technicians were untrained in the procedures. The excessive time was putting patients at risk, so he canceled all such procedures until trained technicians were available. This forced the emergency room to turn away trauma cases that would have needed angiograms and cost the hospital a considerable sum of money. They apparently were not content to end his contract but wanted to get his medical license, I guess as a lesson to others. I got the lesson, so we moved, arriving in late middle-age in the intermountain region. My mother had died by this time after a long period of dementia. . The cousins and uncles and aunts that had once formed an extended family for an only child were left behind.

In the midst of the translocations, I sought the advice of a psychiatric friend. After listening to my tale of woe, he had this observation "Mac, you are amiable and people assume you're flexible and you're not. Secondly, you're a moralist." Well, I guess a Catholic upbringing has some benefits. Your mother had another observation, that I had a restless spirit. She was right, of course. I guess it's no surprise that my favorite Gospel hymn is "Wayfaring Stranger". The end result of this wandering was that I had no attachment to place, institution, or congregation, only to my family, which probably explains why your mother and I hung together for so long. Ultimately, that attachment too ended.

Left behind also was the cultural comfort provided by the Church. The late discovery of the pedophilia scandal was not the trigger. Though I had been an altar boy up to high school, I never had an interaction with a priest or brother that was other than moral. No, it just seemed that a lot of the religious fine points were no longer relevant to me. I guess that arguing religion with your mother for thirty years burned away that passion. It did one other thing. It made me realize that a lot of the intellectual structure that the Church used to explain or defend its belief was flawed. The logic structure is like a mathematical theorem that is based on a postulate that cannot be proven by the theorem. For example, to prove that God exists they assume there cannot be an infinite series of causes and that therefore He must be the uncaused cause. Why can't there be an infinite series of causes? Mathematicians are quite happy to work with the concept of infinity. Fractal theory posits that a finite area can be bounded by a line of infinite length. This is like one of Einstein's thought experiments, Schrödinger's cat in medieval form. Modern empirical science did not destroy the structure but displaced it. People and societies found a new way to knowledge, by seeing, touching and measuring.

Tennyson again:
"The old order changeth yielding place to new
And God fulfills Himself in many ways
Lest one good custom should corrupt the world."

In science was the promise of certainty and predictability, a lovely mechanistic universe in which there was no God to disturb the mechanics. I loved it, the age of Watson and Crick, DNA, allosteric enzymes and metabolic control. It was an exciting time. Of course, as you and I know, the promise was not met. Even when the human genome was deciphered, all we learned was that there were large stretches of DNA that did nothing, and the rest made proteins whose function in many cases was obscure. I should have known better. I should have remembered my physics and physical chemistry. Lurking in the background, unacknowledged, was Einstein's relativity and Heisenberg's uncertainty. And after a while, I was left with neither causality, nor certainty nor the assurance of salvation.

Tennyson yet again:
"Yet all experience is an arch where through
Gleams that untraveled world whose margin fades
Forever and ever when I move"

Sarah's scientific background was no less thorough than mine but she could keep both worlds apart and still live in both. Maybe Saint Paul and maybe Luther were right, that it's all based on faith. But I could not get there myself. I knew now that going back to the old way would not do. Maybe her experience would provide a path, or at least a guide.

The beeper was sounding and the number was that of ICU. I called and the nurse told me that the potential donor had ceased to trigger the respirator and that her pupils were dilated and unresponsive to light. Her time had just about run out. I had been in the physician's dictation room in the back of ICU and walked up front to the young lady's bed. Exactly as reported, she was not triggering the ventilator and her pupils were fixed. I asked the nurse to get a fifty cc irrigating syringe and some ice water. I also asked her to call the respiratory therapist to prepare for an apnea test.

The nurse arranged some towels around the patient's head and then held her eyelids open. When I irrigated the left ear with fifty cc of ice water the eyes did not move. Similar result on the right. Basically, the ice water anesthetizes the balance organ on that side, leaving the other side to drive the eyes to the opposite side. Failure to respond indicates that the eye movement centers in the pons have been destroyed or are non-functional. Since her pupils were fixed to light, I could infer that the mid-brain was non-functional or destroyed. It only remained to test the function of the lowest part of the brainstem, where centers for blood pressure control and respiration were located, and this would require an apnea test.

The respiratory tech cut a length of suction catheter, and attached it to an oxygen source and prepared to thread it down the ET tube. Her previous blood gas measurements showed a CO_2 level that was acceptable for the test. We disconnected her from the machine, put the catheter down the ET tube and started the oxygen flowing at six liters per minute. This would be adequate to keep her blood oxygen up to normal even if she could not breathe. Carbon dioxide is the main stimulus to breathing, and by letting the carbon dioxide accumulate, the function of the respiratory centers in the medulla could be tested.

Once the oxygen was flowing, the clock started, actually the stop watch function on my watch. The nurse watched the monitor above the bed for any signs of cardiac irregularity, while I watched the chest for any sign of respiratory activity. One minute ticked by, then another and another, still no movement or cardiac problem. The tech drew a blood gas sample from the arterial line and then I gave her another five minutes before asking the nurse to pull the catheter out and reconnect the ventilator. I noted the result in the chart along with the blood carbon dioxide level, which was more than adequate to stimulate breathing.

I called the transplant network nurse to let her know the result and ordered a brain blood flow study for the morning to complete the determination. The nurse assured me she was a donor from the statement on her driver's license. I needed to talk to her family, so that they knew and I hoped would understand what was happening. I wasn't sure what I would find. We used to associate methamphetamine use with biker gangs, and I'm told the name crank came from the practice of concealing the drug in the crankcase of a parked, unused motorcycle. As the drug became more popular and its use spread to other socio-economic classes, I never knew who I would meet in the waiting room.

The transplant network nurse had met with the family and had kept them up to date on her course. She had said that they were unsure about the whole idea of organ donation. I looked at the license to double-check the donor section. Yeah, just like mine.

There was an older man, probably mid fifties, wearing a well tailored blue suit, and a middle aged woman, Ann Taylor style, both with the rumpled look of time spent in waiting rooms. There was also a young man, possibly sixteen, in jeans and golf shirt, with a backpack at his feet. I introduced myself, and said "I know this is a very bad time for you. As the nurse told you, the prolonged seizures she suffered caused severe brain damage. I just finished some tests of brainstem activity and there is no function there. Tomorrow, another study will be done to check blood flow to the brain and if there is none, as I suspect, she will be declared dead and the organ donation process will begin.

At this fairly blunt speech, the mother broke down in racking sobs and the boy put his arm around her. The father asked "Why did she do this? Why so much? It wasn't that she didn't know about drugs, she had a degree in chemistry and taught science in high school. Why?"

I said "Meth is the most addictive drug that I know with a long lasting high and a crash when it's gone."

He said "I know that, dammit, why did she start?"

I said, "I don't know for sure, but I can guess that like the rest of us, she did something she knew was wrong to please someone who loved her or said he did."

He said, "He never really loved her."

I replied, "Likely not, but it probably was not that she need to be loved as she needed to love someone."

He asked, "Don't we have some say in this donation business?"

I replied, "Strictly speaking, no, she designated herself a donor when she got her drivers license and did not change the designation when she renewed it last year."

He said, "She was barely eighteen when she got her adult license. I doubt she knew what it meant."

I took a moment before saying, "Eighteen year olds vote, join the military and die for their country; they know what they are doing. But think of it this way, I know it seems like a snap decision when the DMV clerk asks whether you want to be a donor. But the yes springs from the deepest and noblest part of a human person, the desire to benefit others even after your death. She knew what she was doing, and that love and generosity of spirit will be her legacy to you. And because of her decision, five people will live and another will see again."

The mother had stopped sobbing and the father just nodded at me. There was silence.

The nurse and I turned and left the conference room. Outside she said to me "In an earlier life, you must have been a preacher."

I replied "Earlier life my foot, I almost was in this one."

And yes, Kathleen, I did once consider the priesthood, briefly. I didn't, for no reason that I can now recall. What would have been the result if the decision had gone the other way? Well, I probably would not be writing this letter to you while waiting for the Medical Board to make up their collective minds. On the other hand, I might have been like a cousin of mine who entered the seminary out of high school, and was a priest for ten years then left. As he said, loving God was not enough; he had to love another person.

CHAPTER 11

I walked back to the office, and found a message that Weston had called. I dialed his number and he answered. He said, "My wife told me you needed a second opinion on a myasthenic. Who wants it and why?"

I replied "I'm the one who wants you to review and monitor the case."

He asked "Why me and not one of the other neurologists, maybe Dr. Chen who did a fellowship in neuromuscular disease?"

I said "Well, there may be some ethical issues as well as the medical ones."

He asked "Ethical? Is this a family member or close friend?"

"Not initially a close friend but some friendship has developed."

There was a pause, and then he asked "More than a friend?"

I quickly replied "No"

He asked "Really? Who raised the ethical issues?"

I said "Mostly I did."

Quickly he said "Quit and get Chen."

I said somewhat strongly "The patient does not want me to quit."

He asked "But would she, I presume the patient is female, accept a second opinion?"

Quickly "Yes to both questions."

He paused a moment, then said "OK, I have to give a lecture at the school tomorrow. Have all the data in the chart as my passwords have expired and besides, I hate their computer system."

Gratefully I said "I will and thanks."

He continued "I presume that given the ethical issues, you would want me to review from time to time?"

Quickly I said "Definitely."

Finally he said "Alright, I'll call you tomorrow after I see her."

"Thanks again."

After getting Weston involved, I reviewed my message log. In addition to the usual patient problems, the manager had flagged one with a note " Another one of your girlfriends called- Call Susan – no subject" I made the patient calls first, then called Susan. She is an OR nurse, who used to work neurology, until the heavy lifting got to her. She had been at St. James even before I arrived, and knew everybody. She is a widow, whose husband was an alcoholic and a helicopter pilot, manifestly unlucky, since he died in a crash. It was she who asked me to end the support of the hospital nurse who had suffered a stroke after thrombolytic therapy a few months back. Despite my manager's classification, our friendship had been limited to the hospital.

She said, "I saw on the admission list that Sarah is in ICU. Can she have a visitor?"

I replied "Sure, but how do you know her?"

"We grew up together, were in grade and high school together, and I was part of her wedding. We lost touch over the last year or two when she took the job with the resort."

I asked "What can you tell me about her?"

"What do you want to know?"

I was tempted to say "Tell me everything about her." But said, "Tell me what happened in her marriage and what happened in med school."

She paused for a moment then said "Well, first you have to understand her family, her dad was a pharmacist, her mother was a nurse, and her oldest sister went to med school here and now heads a large and profitable biotech firm. There were seven kids, all in Catholic grade school and high school. All went to college, had professional training, married well, supported the Church and were pillars of the community. They floated over life. She went down the same road at first, pre med, married in her senior year of college, med school, babies, and then failure. You know what the first year of med school is like- lectures, labs, and exams every few weeks and the constant peer pressure, you're lucky if you have time to take a piss. The husband was an asshole, wanted her home, didn't want kids, wanted to build his accounting practice, and she broke. Grades dropped, the dean suggested she leave school, and she tried harder but no luck. We met for lunch one Saturday and when she came I saw her left cheek was bruised even though she had covered the mark with makeup. I didn't need to ask what happened. She looked like she had aged ten years. The bright, athletic, funny girl I grew up with was gone and in her place was a worn old woman, with no sparkle, slumped shoulders, and after just seeing her I wanted to cry."

I asked "What happened then?"

She continued "She was so depressed that she couldn't function. She had that thousand-yard stare I used to see in the soldiers back from Nam. The asshole moved out, divorce proceedings started. Her parents took the kids and she spent six weeks in that little hospital down the street from St. James, you know the one I mean."

Briefly, "Yeah."

She added "You know she's bipolar?"

"No, her kids never mentioned it, but I wondered why she was on valproic acid."

She said "Well, that's why."

"Then what", I asked.

"Once she got back to where she could think of the future, she went back to school for a Masters in nutrition, and got a job as a dietician at St. James. She got the house in the divorce along with the mortgage, some child support, and her old Honda wagon. But she was never quite the same. I don't know if it was the medication or the experience but the sparkle and fun were gone."

"What about her family?" I asked.

She said "Well, you know, it's like they thought she wasn't in the same league with her sister, so I'm not sure how close she is to her brothers and sisters. Her father is still around but her mother died of a stroke some years back. Come to think of it, you were the neurologist on the case weren't you?"

I said "Yeah, but I didn't remember the case until her kids mentioned it" Then "How come she didn't remarry?"

She thought for a moment then said "I think she didn't trust herself, and then there was the Church thing. Even though for years she didn't practice, she still had a Catholic soul. And then, the prospects out there are not exciting. You know, guys are divorced for a reason, and picking one is like buying a used car, like, whose trouble are you getting? I think I've met most of them. How about you? You live alone, and you never asked me out."

I said "I had the phone in my hand once or twice."

She said "What happened?"

"I figured you'd have better sense than to accept. Besides, nothing spoils a friendship like romance."

She said "I could stand being spoiled for a while. But all you do is work. You make drying paint seen exciting."

I thought I'd better change the subject, so I asked "What about her kids, how much do they depend on her?"

She replied "Not a lot now, the girl is a senior in the university; the boy is a skilled mechanic with his own shop. I think the father gives them some support, like cars and tuition, but not much emotional support."

"Does she have any male friends now?" I asked.

She said "Not that she has mentioned to me. She did meet a guy at church about two years ago, that she really liked but it turned out he was married and she could not take the responsibility for breaking up a marriage, so she broke it off."

I said, mostly to myself, "Sounds familiar."

She continued "Huh? Well anyway, she doesn't have anybody at this time. But your curiosity makes me think your interests are more than professional."

I said, "I'm not sure how I feel, but there is a generation between us, so it's more like my feeling for my daughters, but not exactly the same".

She said "For your sake, I hope it's more than that. You need to love again."

With a smile I said, "You mean my dogs are not enough?"

She shook her head, "No, nor are mine for me. You know, I remember from one of my high school religion classes with Sarah, a Bible verse that said 'One who does not love abides in death'. I wish we could have been more than friends because both of us are a bit dead."

I shook my head "I don't know if I could be more than that for anyone. Anyway, thanks for the information. Feel free to visit with her any time."

She gave me a hug and turned away.

When I walked through ICU the next morning, there was a note on the front of Sarah's chart from Weston saying "Call me at home." In the progress notes he had scrawled an indecipherable note that I barely managed to decipher "History reviewed, patient examined, labs reviewed, note dictated." Nothing more. I checked the back of the chart but the dictation was not back yet and was not yet in the computer.

I called him from the nursing station. His wife answered first and then he came on the line. I said "Thanks for the review. Your dictation is not back yet."

He said "Thank you for requesting me to do this, I was starting to get bored and needed a challenge. First of all, she is a nice person that I remember from when I was teaching first year students, and I wondered what had happened to her. I think I also taught her sister. That one was the family star, possibly the smartest woman I ever met. I heard she heads a biotech company. Sarah tried to meet the family standard. I was on the committee that reviewed her first year performance and recommended that she take a leave of absence. We hoped she could come back when her personal problems were corrected. We hate to lose good students. Anyway, here is what I think. The clinical history and your electrical studies are consistent with myasthenia gravis. But she is not responding to the plasmaphoresis and steroids and pyridostigmine as I would expect. Also, the blocking and binding antibodies are negative. I doubt this is Lambert-Eaton syndrome on the basis of the nerve conduction studies, and the fact that those antibodies are also negative."

Surprised, I said, "I didn't think those were back yet."

He went on "They're not; I called Mayo Clinic to get the results. Still, I think you should do the high frequency stimulation studies to make sure. If those are negative, then she has sero-negative myasthenia gravis, which fits her clinical picture best. It is more common in women this age, affects the respiratory and bulbar muscles most and does not respond well to acetylcholine esterase inhibitors. Exactly what is going on in this form of the disease is unclear, but probably there is an antibody to some component of the muscle other than the endplate region. The limited studies in the literature suggest that plasmaphoresis or high dose immune globulin infusion may work, but the outcome is worse than for the garden-variety myasthenia. Why the first series has not produced the rapid response that I would expect is not clear, but probably she is producing the antibody almost as fast as the phoresis removes it. You might want to add another immunosuppressive agent, either cytoxan or cyclosporine to the steroids when you do the second series. Also she will need a tracheotomy and feeding tube soon. One more thing, she is counting on you to get her through this, and while she has no problem with me, she wants you on the case to end, and maybe beyond. You need to think about what to do if we fail her. How much do you know about her? What does she want from life? How much does the personal relationship affect her? How much does it affect you?"

I said "That's a lot of questions. I don't know enough about her yet. About failure, I'd rather not think about that now."

His voice got a bit harsh "Well, OK, for now, but remember she likes you and trusts you to serve her interests and your personal feelings for her have got to be put aside."

He spoke sharply when I said "I understand."

He continued "Do you? There may be some hard decisions to come that neither of us will like. You asked me to review this case for ethical reasons, and that was right. But any competent neurologist would have thought through this case as you have. You really want me to watch your back, and I'm happy to do that. But she insists on you staying on the case, and that's only partly because of friendship. She wants you to be able to do the hard stuff if and when the time comes and not to drift away if it comes to her death. Too many docs psychologically abandon their patients who are dying, and you must not do that, no matter what."

I said "I think I knew that but thanks for spelling it out. I understand the moral obligation, but the emotional side is still undefined. I can't thank you enough for coming on the case. I feel better knowing you will be looking over my shoulder"

He said "I'll come by on a weekly basis and write a note. Feel free to call if you want to talk it over between visits."

CHAPTER 12

I knew that the first thing I had to do was the electrical study that Weston had suggested. For that, I had to talk to Sarah and explain the procedure. The next morning, I sat down at her bedside. The tube feedings were running, and she had some color to her face. I had secured the EMG machine from the basement of the hospital and pushed it into the room. She looked at it and rolled her eyes slightly. I said "Sorry Ms. Smith, but Dr. Weston recommended one additional study." She nodded. I said "This will be brief, but uncomfortable." She picked up the whiteboard and wrote "= painful?" I had to laugh.

"You know me too well."

She wrote "Not yet."

I said "I'll give you a brief but intense electrical stimulus to the median nerve. It will last a second but will seem longer. Can I proceed?'

She nodded.

I put the electrodes on the muscles at the base of the thumb and the stimulator on the wrist. It took two individual shocks to set the stimulator to the proper level, and then I set the stimulator to fifty per second, just slightly below the frequency of house current.

I asked "Ready?"

She nodded. I triggered the stimulator for one second. Her body stiffened and she bit down on the ET tube. Her thumb was rigid and then relaxed. Sweat broke out on her face. The high frequency stimulus clearly distinguishes myasthenia gravis from Eaton –Lambert syndrome because in the latter, the response starts out low and builds, and in the former, the response starts high and drops. We don't use it routinely since it is like sticking your finger in a light socket. Her response was typical of myasthenia gravis.

I said, as I took the electrode off "I'm sorry that hurt so much, I hate this test."

I said "This definitely proves you have myasthenia gravis. But your antibody tests are negative. This probably means that we are not measuring the right antibody. So I'll continue the plasma phoresis and add an additional agent to suppress antibody formation. Also, I'll arrange for a tracheostomy and feeding tube placement which will make you much more comfortable. I'll try to arrange for a tracheostomy device that will enable you to talk a bit."

She wrote "OK, do it. Now how long do I have?"

I said "At least two weeks for the next plasmaphoresis, and then, I'm not sure."

She wrote "Weston?"

I replied "He thinks that sero-negative myasthenia is more difficult to treat, but the literature is unclear on the exact course to follow."

She wrote "Weston said ethics problem."

I said "Well, yes in a sense. A problem of affection."

She wrote "Who?"

I said "You"

She wrote "Meaning?"

I said "I think that you have developed a feeling of affection for me."

She wrote "Yeah and?"

I said "I think I have the same problem."

She wrote "You like you?"

I laughed "No, you know what I mean."

Small smile.

She wrote "Yes, glad. Better like than not."

I said "But if my judgment is impaired, the best thing to do would be to withdraw from the case."

She wrote "My right"

Puzzled, I said "What do you mean?"

She wrote "I decide when or if. Right?"

I said "Yes, that's your right."

She wrote "Stay"

With a smile, I said "My pleasure Madam."

"Me too"

She took my hand and interlaced her fingers with mine and we both just looked at each other for a while.

After a bit, I said "I talked to Susan yesterday before she visited with you. She told me a lot about your marriage and after. You really had a bad time."

She let go of my hand to write "Past. Now, now is all. Talk to me about you."

I said "Well, like you two adult children, both doing well. I was married for a long time. Wife moved on, career and well, maybe accumulated differences, partly religious."

She wrote "Divorce?'

Briefly, I said "No, still Catholic a bit."

She wrote "Girlfriend?'

I shook my head saying "No."

She wrote "Have one now."

I said "Good thing you like them old."

She wrote "Mature"

I said "Only wine and whiskey get better with age."

She wrote "Friendship also"

There was a long pause and then I said, "I need to get back to business. Tomorrow I'll ask the surgeons to see you about the tracheostomy and I'll ask the nephrologists to plan on a second series. Also I'll start you on cyclosporine and decrease the steroids before you look like a chipmunk."

"OK" she wrote, then "Pray for me"

I said "I will if I remember how. Don't be scared"

"I am. Prayer doesn't need words. Stay with me for a bit"

I held her hand for a few minutes and then she closed her eyes and let go of my hand.

She went to surgery the following morning. The informed consent was signed by her and cosigned by her daughter. The daughter had called me to talk about the progress. She was concerned about how slowly her mother was recovering. There was, I felt an undertone of negativity or perhaps hostility in her voice. I went over the data and Weston's review and tried to explain the significance of the sero-negative status. I tried to be reassuring but I think she detected the uncertainty in my presentation.

She said, "Mom hasn't had male friends in a couple of years. The men she has known proved disappointing. My Dad's not much support. There is still a lot of bad feeling there, at least on his side. She sees you as more than her doctor."

That explained the hostility I sensed. She wanted her mother protected in addition to being cured. Unless I wanted to get caught between the mother and the daughter, this would have to be resolved quickly.

I said, "She's more than just a patient as far as I'm concerned. We have become friends. . I recognize that there is an element of vulnerability here. Having a second opinion is a safeguard on my judgment. Once she is better, I would hope the friendship could continue. Her religious beliefs are consistent with mine." We parted with my promise to keep her up to date. I must confess that I have never been good at false optimism and facile assurances that all will be well. I know damn well they may not be.

Sarah was back in ICU at noon, with tracheostomy in place and feeding tube in her upper abdomen now concealed beneath her gown. Although still slightly sedated she looked like a queen about to receive visitors. .The nurses had brushed her hair and put on some lipstick and a bit of makeup. When I came to the bedside, I got smile undistorted by tubes. The trach did not have a speaking valve because the pulmonary physicians did not think she could be off the ventilator support long enough to talk. Still, she appeared to be much more comfortable.

She wrote "How do I look?"

I said, "Beautiful, seeing you makes my day."

She wrote, "Come close."

As I bent over her she pulled my face to hers and kissed me on the cheek. Then she wrote "I hope you don't mind"

I said "Mind? I wish I'd thought of it first. But do you always greet you doctors this way?"

She wrote "No. Just my friends"

I asked, "How does the throat feel?"

She wrote "Sore as is the nose but I feel more human."

I said, "Hopefully, once the breathing improves, they will fit a valve to let you talk."

She wrote "You may not want a woman who talks."

I replied "There are a lot of things I'd like to talk with you about when we have the time"

She wrote "Tomorrow-not promised. We start now."

I said "OK, but the last time you questioned me, I thought about it for a week."

She wrote, "Not sorry. I want to know you. And you me."

I asked "Tell me how you got back to the Church."

She took her time writing "Bottomed out. Had a job, kids doing OK, but was still a failure, empty, surviving just. The old faith was ritual, family tradition, incense and the rosary. When everything fell apart, that went too."

I asked, "You went back on Good Friday, why that day?"

She wrote, "It was a day of failure, pain, suffering, and death." She stopped writing for a moment, wiped off the first line and then wrote "And a victory of faith."

I asked "Faith? How do you mean?"

She wrote "Faith = trust. Not belief."

I asked "You mean despite the failure and certainty of death, He still trusted the Father to bring Him through?"

She wrote, "Right" and then stopped for a moment. Then she wrote "In my despair, I saw Him as a Person who knew what I was feeling."

There was a long pause then I said "I remember I once had a similar feeling, but it didn't last. Still, there may be echoes in my memory."

She wrote "Explain please."

I said, "It was a long time ago, maybe thirty, forty years. I was in a similar state of mind. I was in graduate school, my father had died, my research project had crashed and I had broken an engagement. Probably for the first time, I had a sense of utter failure as a person and an overwhelming sense of guilt. There was no place to go to escape myself and my sense of failure as a person. From somewhere out of the past, I recalled the next to last words, 'Why have you forsaken me' and understood that He felt as I felt."

She quickly wrote "So why doubt now?"

I had to think back. "I guess that the emotional impact did not last. That would be too much to expect, like trying to sustain the fires of romance through a long marriage. Then life happened. Jobs, children, a marriage, financial problems all seemed more important. A seemingly endless struggle. And then there is the practice. I guess other specialties like family practice, peds, have a sunnier outlook, but I see a lot of degenerative disease and intracranial disasters. I've been at this for almost thirty years and not much has changed. It's an unremitting series of bad things and mostly futile therapy, and any victory is temporary. Mind you, I don't blame God, that's just the way the world is. I might as well blame God for gravity or sunshine. I may be able to make a person's life a bit better for a time. But nothing seems to last. It seems the default position of the world is chaos and death."

She wrote, "Why not quit?"

"What else would I do? I take care of people, I've done research and it wasn't satisfying. Even though I don't think unremitting, futile labor is noble, it is work I can do and do reasonably well. Doing a job well is a source of satisfaction. So I do it, and occasionally I'm rewarded with the chance to meet and know people like you."

She wrote "Despite that, is there still an echo?"

"Yeah, there is, in a way. I think that at some point He realized that the human part of His mission would end in a bloody failure. Yet He pushed on. And I wonder if in some part of His human soul, there was a particle of doubt that He would come through transcendent. You know, if you're God for whom the past, the present, and the future is all now, it's easy. But if you're a man, it's not."

She wrote "Man? Sexist."

I said "I meant that generically."

I noted that her notes were shorter and she was having trouble holding the marker.

She wrote one more note, folded it and pushed it to me and motioned me to come closer.

I bent over her and she reached for me. I kissed her on the forehead and got a weak smile. As I stepped away, I took the note and unfolded it outside her room. It was a number 139.

CHAPTER 13

I assumed that since our last conversation had a religious theme, the number probably had that significance. I once told her I had read the Bible, so she might have assumed that was a current practice of mine. I had meant the past tense. If I were to figure out what she wanted me to know, I would have to root through boxes of books to find my old Bible.

Meanwhile, the tech was preparing the plasmaphoresis machine for the second treatment series. I reviewed her lab work, talked briefly with the nurses, who seemed to know without my saying, how I felt. They usually don't miss a thing. I had a full office schedule, so did not get back to ICU till late evening. Sarah was asleep. I looked at her for a long moment and then left.

I fed the dogs and threw their toys for them, and then went into the garage and looked through book boxes until the Bible turned up. It had been a few years since it had been opened and the marker was still on the page holding Psalm 13.

"How long, O Lord? Will you forget me forever?
How long will you hide your face from me?

How long must I bear pain in my soul, and have sorrow in my heart all day long?"

I recalled that that was how I felt for months after, a very brief, chaste but intense relationship a few years back. It had taken a while to pack away the emotions along with the Bible. I wondered whether I could stand that again. Back at the kitchen table, I flipped back to Psalm 139, realizing that it had been some time since I had read it. Since you had a Bible class in that Catholic high school that you and your sister attended, you're probably familiar with this Psalm.

The psalmist, maybe David, elaborates on the overwhelming presence of God, Who is present wherever we are, even in the realm of the dead, Sheol, and He knows our life before it begins and after it ends. There are some beautiful lines in this translation, such as "If I take the wings of morning and fly to the farthest reaches of the sea, you are there."

I have thought, once in a while, that it would be good to fly to the farthest reaches of the sea, away from the person I have become. But what was it she was trying to tell me that she could not convey with her limited writing? Was she trying to tell me she felt the presence of God all around, or that she was comforted that her life's course was known and determined and would end with her in the presence of God? Or was this meant to help me with my own doubts?

I have an elderly patient that I inherited from another physician, and this old man was a runner until his knees protested. Now he was the caregiver for his wife who was blind from diabetes and had multiple sclerosis. At one visit, while he was waiting, I saw him reading from an anthology of poetry. Curious, I asked him why and which poem. The poem was the "Hound of Heaven" by Francis Thompson and he was memorizing it to keep his mind sharp. By coincidence, I too had once memorized the opening stanzas, which we recited together. He continued for another five stanzas .It was a lovely symmetry of two minds. I can still recall the opening lines "I fled Him, down the nights and down the days;
I fled Him, down the arches of the years;

I fled Him, down the labyrinthine ways
Of my own mind;"

Recalling that scene, I wondered, with the Psalm, was she trying to tell me that fleeing God was futile? Or that both our lives were foreseen and determined. I was not prepared to accept the last, at least while there was some option.

I suspected that, now that Sarah had her tracheostomy, there would be some pressure to move her out of ICU. Thus it was no surprise that Davidson stopped me the next morning and asked me to agree to a move to the neurology ward. He promised that the nurses would be skilled in managing the ventilator and that there would be no problem with the plasmaphoresis. I agreed, provided that she could get a private room. Davidson was desperate to clear an ICU bed and so we had a deal. She was moved to neurology that morning, and given a private room on the East side with a view of the mountains and the sunrise. Her family brought in a lot of pictures and cards and taped them to the wall where she could see them. Since this is an old hospital, the rooms are small, but the nurses had managed to squeeze in one comfortable chair in addition to the usual variety that discourages visitors from a long stay.

On my lunch break, I went to her room, and found her in a semi-sitting position, with head of the bed elevated. The nurses had brushed her hair and applied a bit of makeup and a touch of lipstick. She looked like a queen receiving her courtiers, of which I was one. When I walked through the door, she motioned me over to the bed, raised her arms to me and enfolded me in a hug and a kiss, and not just on the forehead. She motioned me over to the chair, and took up her marker and white board. She wrote "Nicer room, better view."

I replied "Glad to be of service. Is there anything else I can do for you?"

She wrote "Yeah, 139 did you read?"

I said "Yes, I did. Why did you suggest this one?"

She wrote "It tells you about me."

I asked "Which means that you feel your life is determined or that God envelops you?"

She wrote "Both. What about you?"

I said "I recalled reading it some time ago and was struck by the verses about taking the wings of morning and settling at the farthest limits of the sea. That drew me somehow."

She wrote "Why?"

I looked out the window and said "Well, the practice is a bit grim and I have become both cynical and cold. Mostly I insulate myself from the losses around me. I guess most physicians do that as a survival technique. But the emotional parts of me die a little bit more each year. I think I mean that I'd like to get back to the person I was years ago, more free and perhaps more childlike and maybe with more hope."

She wrote "More faith?"

I said "Maybe too much to expect."

She wrote "Why? Faith is trust."

I said "Sounds too simple.'

She wrote "Is simple but not easy. Doubt is easy." And underlined it. Then she laid the marker down and looked at me for a moment. She waved me to come closer. I saw that she was crying silently. I went over to her and put my arm around her. She put her head on my shoulder.

I said, "Look, I'm sorry I was so negative. It was wrong to lay all that despair on you like that."

She shook her head and laid a finger across my lips as if to say "Shut up." So I did.

She lay quiet a moment, then took up the whiteboard and the marker and wrote "I asked. You shared. How else to know?"

At that point, my beeper went off, as it had at other significant points in my life. I said "Damn"

She smiled, and kissed me on the cheek. I said, "I'll come back this afternoon." She nodded.

Chapter 14

The number on the pager was the ED and appended was the code for urgent response. I found a house phone and dialed the clerk, who answered "St. James emergency department, this is Sally. How may I help you?" I responded "Dr. Mac--, you paged me." She said "One moment for Dr. Bannister." Bannister came on the line "Mac, you're not gonna believe this. We had a shooting in the waiting room. Get down here. We have a gunshot wound to the head in status epilepticus. I gotta go." Click.

It was faster to use the stairs and as I entered the hallway, two uniformed cops pushed past me. Going through the automatic doors, I was struck by how quiet the place was. At the monitor tech's cubicle was a hand lettered sign "ER DIVERT" meaning that all ambulances were to be directed to the hospital across town. The tech barely looked up as I approached and said, "Room three" and then went back to staring at her screens. Down the corridor to room three, I could see through the open doors to the waiting room. The area was guarded by uniformed cops and hospital security. The space in front of the triage clerk's vacant desk was marked by yellow tape. There was only one small spot of blood on the tiles and a paper marker for the location of what appeared to be a spent cartridge.

The patient on the gurney was a middle-aged man. He had been intubated. The ventilator was on the left and IV pumps were on the right. The patient's right thumb was twitching about once a second. As I watched, the twitching increased in frequency then spread to the other fingers, then to the wrist and forearm. When the twitching reached the corner of the mouth, his head and eyes jerked to the left. In an instant, he was in a full-blown Grand mal seizure, back arched and eyes open and rolled up. The nurse turned and said, "That's the third in ten minutes."

I asked, "How much phenytoin is in?"

She said, "Almost all of the twelve hundred milligrams."

I said, "It's not working. Give him six milligrams of midazolam and start a drip of six milligrams per hour."

She went to get the drug and put the order in the computer.

I went to take a closer look. The left side of his head was perfectly intact. On the right side, just above and forward of the ear was a dressing, stained with blood and clear fluid. A very brief exam showed that he did not respond to pain and his pupils still were equal and reacted to light. I estimated his Glasgow coma scale at three to four, which was just what the nurse's notes showed. When the nurse returned with the medication, I went to the nursing station to review the CT scan and the chart.

The CT scan was slow in appearing, and as I looked through the chart, the head nurse came up to me and said, "I can save you some time. Here's the story. He walked up to the triage desk, handed over his insurance card and his driver's license with the donor status circled in red. When the clerk turned to get an admission packet, he put a gun to his head and shot himself. The clerk freaked. Luckily, there were only a few people in the waiting room. I heard the shot and thought we were having another gang shooting. We called a code gray, but it was over before security arrived. Neurosurgery saw him and reviewed the CT. Do look at the chest film."

I said, "What?"

She said, "You'll see." And walked away.

The neurosurgical note was brief- No operative intervention, seizure control.

The CT scan told the story in part. On the right side there was a small hole in the skull with radiating fracture lines and bone fragments in the tissue. Under the hole was a cavity filled with blood and a track leading to the left side and then back to the right on a diagonal. About one inch from the inner aspect of the skull on the right, the projectile had come to rest, a partially deformed .22. I had the unworthy thought that if he had used a bigger caliber, he would have saved us a lot to trouble. But then something else caught my eye. There was a small lucency in the frontal area of the skull bone that was abnormal, possibly Paget's disease or- I pulled up the chest film and saw what the head nurse had seen. There was a tissue density in the left upper lobe that could only be a lung cancer.

I went up to ICU to check on the effect of the midazolam on his seizures. The seizure activity was mostly controlled except for some random twitches of his left thumb. The social worker assigned to the case had tracked down, with the aid of the police, a good bit of his history. He was a Vietnam vet with an honorable discharge but had not done well after his service. He could not sustain relationships, hold a job, or handle alcohol. For a while, he had lived on the street, and lately in a religious shelter. He got some of his care at the VA and at the county clinic. That was where his original cancer diagnosis was made. The staff said that he did not return to the clinic even though they were trying to arrange for chemotherapy by the VA. The shelter staff noticed that he was withdrawn the last few weeks, and were going to arrange for counseling when he appeared to be better and more talkative. That was a day or two before he came to the ED. He left no note, and no one could recall any discussion of suicide. He was a solitary man and made his decision in solitude. I can only speculate that he wanted to get things right for once and thus made the noble but unknowingly futile decision to make a gift of himself. Apparently, the social worker had found some records indicating that he was or had been Catholic, and had asked the chaplain to see him. Without delay, Fr. Francis had been by, and administered the Sacrament of the Sick.

I added an additional anti-convulsant medication, and ordered an EEG, mostly to see how much cortical function remained. The neurosurgeons and trauma surgeons had scheduled a conference for the next morning and had asked for an ethics committee meeting to decide his care in the absence of family guidance. He could not be an organ donor due to the metastatic cancer, so the issue would be futility of further care. The ethics committee can be assembled quickly as the members including Fr. Frances were on campus. There would have to be an oncologist to opine about treatment of his cancer and probably my opinion about his intellectual function. All of this could be done on the following day and then, if futility was the consensus, and no family was available, support would be terminated.

The second plasmaphoresis series was about half completed, Sarah's pulmonary function tests had not budged above sixty percent of normal and would decline between series. She was having a treatment this morning, and instead of dozing through it as usual, she was staring out the window as I arrived. She motioned me to the bedside, took up the whiteboard and wrote"Look to the east, just north of the airport." I looked where she indicated and at first did not see any thing but sky and sagebrush. Then following her gaze I saw them, two hawks floating on the thermals or riding the updrafts before the foothills. Several species of hawks inhabit this area, but red tails are the most common, and despite the distance that's what they looked like to me. I would have thought that our sagebrush desert would not be a prime habitat, but the city provides trees and power-poles and the hawks, like the Marines, prefer to take the high ground. They were flying a large circle at one hundred eighty degrees to each other. Whether they were hunting or simply enjoying the late fall day, I could not tell, but most of the pigeons and gulls had wisely cleared out.

She took my hand and we watched them for a few minutes before they drifted out of our field of view. She lay back and took up the whiteboard and marker and wrote "The wings of morning, I know what you mean."

I said "Yes a degree of freedom that we can't experience but long for."

She wrote "Can't go back"

I said "No time travel, time flows one way."

After a moment she wrote "I'm not getting much better am I?"

I shook my head "No, the procedures are holding you at about sixty percent of normal."

She wrote "Is there anything else?"

I said "If the plasmaphoresis doesn't work, I'll try an infusion of gamma globulin that may reset your immune system. It works well for Guillian-Barre, and for some other autoimmune disorders."

She wrote "I wish I could talk to you. This system is too limited." She waved the marker.

I said "Let me talk to the speech people, there may be a way to fit the trach with a valve that would allow some speech."

She wrote "Please do, I need to talk to you. Writing is limited. But I'm afraid."

She took her time carefully printing the words, and pushed the board to me.

I said "Afraid? Of what?"

She wrote, "Of getting better or not"

I said "I don't understand."

She wrote, "If I get better, will I just be another patient?'

I said "No, I'm selfish. I hope we can be closer than that. You started me thinking about things that I haven't considered for over twenty years. It's like trying to get back home. You may have the map."

She wrote "Home?"

I said "Home. Well that's a place in my mind that's comfortable and familiar, a place where it possible to love and believe. Not the ritual and the incense. "

She motioned me closer and raised her arms. I kissed her and held her for a moment. She lay back and closed her eyes and a tear trickled down her cheeks. I left.

I went down to speech therapy to ask them to reconsider the valve for the trach. At sixty percent of normal lung function she was on the edge of being able to come off the respirator for a limited period of time but the therapists wanted the pulmonary specialists to weigh in on the decision. So I went to find Davidson who was in charge of ICU that month. He was in the dictation room, reviewing lab data.

He greeted me, saying, "Morning Mac how's the lady?

I said "Better, but not good enough. I want to talk about her."

He looked up and said "OK, let's see the data."

He entered her patient number and brought up her pulmonary function data.

He said "Damn, she was close to dead at first, but now up to sixty percent of normal. But it looks like she is on a plateau. At this level she will at least be partially respirator dependent She is not behaving like a typical myasthenic patient."

I replied "No, she is not typical, the antibody studies are negative."

He shook his head "What does that mean?"

I said, "Nobody really knows. Weston's thought is that the antibody is directed against some intracellular component. That makes it difficult for plasmaphoresis to remove it completely."

He said "So is sixty percent as good as you can get?"

I replied "So far. I may try immune globulin if this series doesn't get us far enough. But what I wanted to discuss is the possibility of a talking valve for the trach. She wants to talk to me and I suppose to her family and she finds the marker and whiteboard too limiting. What do you think?"

He thought for a moment and said "We could fit the valve, but her talking would be limited because she would be off the ventilator to use the valve and given these numbers, she could get into trouble in fifteen minutes or so. We would have to monitor her blood oxygen while she was off the ventilator."

I said, "I think she would accept that."

He said "OK, I'll set it up. Now, what about you? I noticed that you have spent a lot more time on this case. You have been closer to this patient than you cerebral neurologists usually get. How involved are you?"

Cautiously I said, "Well, we have had some discussions about faith and religion."

He said, "Oh, that. Never thought you had an inclination that way. But then you always seem pretty private."

I said, "Was in another life. Old history."

He turned back to the computer and picked up the phone saying "Right, well, I'll tell the speech people to set up the valve and we will monitor her when she is off the blower."

I said "Thanks. See you later."

As I walked back to the neuroscience ward, I realized that as close as we had come, over the past four weeks, that I had never heard her voice except the soft whisper in the emergency room. I remembered the terror in her eyes. I can't imagine what it is like to die of slow suffocation, but I think she knows. My ALS patients also know and together we make a deal. Either choose the respirator or not but no one deserves to die of suffocation. Dying of renal failure seems easier as coma ensues, likewise hepatic failure. Even pure oxygen deficiency is easy as my experience in the high altitude chamber proved. At forty thousand feet, consciousness lasts twenty seconds without the pressure mask.

I walked by her room on my rounds on neuroscience, and saw that she was reading the standard hospital Bible. Probably given by the Gideons. She saw me and waved me over to the bedside. "Read Isa 40:31." She wrote and passed it to me. Then "Valve?"

I said "The speech therapists will fit the valve but we will have to monitor you when it's in place as you will be off the ventilator. I don't know how many minutes you will be able to use the valve, we will just have to see how it goes. Also, does Isa mean Isaiah?

Nod

I shook my head, "Great, more homework."

Smile.

She wrote, "What do you do for fun?"

I replied "Well, I walk one of the dogs up in the hills, cross country ski in winter, read. I used to hunt but no more."

She wrote "Water ski?"

I had to think back "Once about fifty years ago when I was in high school. Never since."

She wrote "Every summer, Dad has ski boat."

I asked, "What do you do in the winter?"

She wrote "Ski, snowshoe."

I said, "You grew up here. I think every child born here learns to ski before they learn to walk."

She wrote "Took flying lessons, almost ready to solo. Loved it."

I asked, "Wasn't that scary?"

She wrote "At first, then fun."

I asked "When you are better, will you go back to the lessons?"

She wrote "Maybe. Depends on strength."

I said "When I was in the service, I had to work with pilots and so, the command thought I should be part of the team. So I had to qualify to fly in the back seat of the F-4 Phantom. I went through the whole bit, high altitude chamber, ejection seat training, and water survival. I remember the final instructions. Do what the pilot says and don't touch anything. Good thing I never flew with them. Probably would have thrown up all over the cockpit."

She was shaking with silent laughter.

CHAPTER 15

The speech therapists placed the valve the following morning, taught Sarah how to use it, and taught the nurses how to monitor her breathing strength. Basically the cuff on the trach was deflated and the respirator disconnected. She would breathe in through the trach, but on exhaling the one way valve would divert air through the larynx permitting speech. It would take some practice as the valve induces more resistance in the system. I did not know how much of her experience in the ED she remembered, as the drug used in the intubations wipes away memory. If she experienced shortness of breath while using the valve, she might have some panic.

I saw her at ten AM, just after they had finished the training. Her voice was soft and a bit hoarse but she managed to say "Good morning love. Sit beside me. Did you read Isaiah? Advent starts soon."
This is the passage she referred to:
"Those who wait for the Lord shall renew their strength
They shall mount up with wings like eagles
They shall run and not be weary
They shall walk and not faint"

I said "I did read it but, tell me what it means."

She said, "To me it means that the Lord will restore my strength now or later, and I have to trust that He will do this. I will wait. What does it mean to you?"

I said, "I suppose I'm waiting as well. For something, I don't know what."

She said, "Perhaps someone to lead you or take you by the hand. The nurses said that you have been alone for a number of years. Tell me what happened to your marriage. You know about mine. "

I stared out the window to the mountains while I thought about her question. Finally, I said, "You grew up in a large family where somebody was always around. And, I guess, that that was pretty much true up through college here and your marriage. I was an only child and only children learn to be alone, by necessity. The psychologists say only children tend to be high achievers and sensitive to criticism from adults. Probably true for me. I was never much interested in money or power. My sin was to love the wrong people and not to love the right people enough. I buried myself in my profession and neglected to develop the necessary relationship with my children or my wife. The children did reasonably well without my being in their lives every minute. Lately I've thought of my marriage rather like two strands of DNA held together by hydrogen bonds. The paired bases share electrons on a statistical basis rather than being locked together in a covalent bond that completes their outer shells of electrons. It doesn't take much to disrupt the hydrogen bonds and then the two strands unwind and set about the business of trying to find or make a new complementary strand. My wife went her own way as did I in several senses. The religious differences were more than some disagreement about some point of theology. No, there is a significant cultural difference, particularly with Southern Protestants. I should have paid more attention to this issue thirty years ago, but then I didn't think it mattered. And for a number of years it didn't. Children came, careers progressed. Then things began to go wrong. She became more church centered and I became less. Since we could not come together on religion, there was a cultural gulf that was always there no matter what we did agree on.

Eventually, I think, my emotional distance was too much for her. I blame myself for the failure. I think the Church would call that a sin of omission."

She said "That business about the DNA is BS. It was your choice or series of choices that brought you here. The path to God goes through love and by failing to love you wandered away from the path to God. Even though you may have sinned, it's not mortal till the failure to love is irreversible. You know the way back. Your choices matter, even when you can't see the path. Now I'm getting short of breath, so call the nurse to hook me back up, but don't leave yet. You and I have much more to do."

I called the nurse who checked her oxygen saturation, nodded and reconnected the ventilator.

She took my hand and lay back for a minute or two. Then she took up the whiteboard and marker and wrote "Damn, I wanted more time."

I wanted more time as well, as much as I could get with her.

She had been without ventilator support for about an hour, which was not going to be enough for a reasonable life. I needed to find a way to boost her strength, by tinkering with the medications, or by some other means. I planned to talk to Weston again, if he had not done his promised case review. I was becoming concerned that I would not be able to wean her from the ventilator. Worse, I could not foresee what lifelong dependency would do to her spirit. I have some ALS patients who, when their respiratory ability failed went on with their lives as much as possible. I recall one physician who was an amateur painter and continued his art with a brush in his teeth. On the other hand, I have seen chronic illness destroy the spirit as well as the body; the patient becoming angry, depressed and self-absorbed and isolated from family and friends. I did not know her well enough to predict her response and didn't really want to find out.

When I got back to the office, there were two messages flagged. The first said call Dr. Davidson ASAP, the second said call Susan. I called Davidson first. He wanted me to attend the ethics committee meeting that afternoon. Susan was in the operating room and unreachable, so I left a message that I had returned her call. The ethics committee meeting was in two hours, leaving me some time to see office patients.

As you will learn Katie, office practice is mostly routine. Check the labs, quick exam, refill medications, answer questions is the usual pattern. As I have aged, so have my patients. Most of their problems have no permanent solution, diseases progress, the medications only buy time. So, it often turns out to be a meeting of old friends to talk over the mutual problems of aging. I think of some lines of Yeats
"An aged man is but a paltry thing,
A tattered coat upon a stick, unless
Soul clap its hands and sing, and louder sing
For every tatter in its mortal dress,"

I had escorted the last old couple from the exam room, when the front desk clerk handed me the phone saying "Susan Somebody wants to talk to you. She is returning your call."
I thought, "Gee, only one round of phone tag." I took the phone saying, "Hey, it's been a while." She didn't waste any time saying "I know you're busy, but I need to talk to you about Sarah, specifically about you and Sarah. Can you meet me today? We have only one more short case this afternoon."
I said, "Let's meet in the cafeteria after my meeting, say 4:45? Should I be worried?"
She said, "I can't discuss over this phone."
I could hear voices in the background, suggesting she was calling from the recovery room. I said, "Good. I'll be there."

The ethics committee met in the small ICU conference room. It was as small as most of the utility rooms on the wards. Since there was a sink in the back of the room, it probably had been a utility room in its past. There was a small table and maybe three chairs, meaning most participants would stand and thus a short meeting. Fr. Francis had one of the chairs and was holding his left forearm with the right hand to control the resting tremor. I had suspected he had Parkinson's disease from seeing him in the hallways. Davidson had one of the other chairs, as did the head nurse from ICU. Davidson opened the meeting with a brief synopsis of the case, including the event in the ED, the lung cancer, and the subsequent course. One of the University oncologists gave his estimate that chemotherapy would provide two months of very bad existence and recommended palliation. It was my turn, and I presented the most recent CT scan showing the tissue damage and the increasing cerebral edema. I said that I thought he would not last the week, absent neurosurgical intervention, which I did not recommend. The nurse said there was no family and except for the press, there were no calls from friends. Davidson said, "I presume, then that the consensus is that further support is futile?" I nodded in agreement as did the nurse and Fr. Francis. The oncologist said, "Hell, his whole life has been futile, he was in the wrong war and made a mess after." I felt my anger rise when Fr. Francis finally spoke. His Irish brogue had more impact because it was so soft, barely above a whisper. He said, "No, 'twas not futile. He made a noble gesture and that is his redemption." There was silence. I thought that was why Fr. Francis gave the sacrament to a probable suicide. I guess the Church had changed since my day. Damn good thing.

Susan was waiting for me in the back of the cafeteria, warming her hands on a mug of tea. She still had on the OR scrubs and wore the heavy support hose that nurses who stand all day adopt despite the old lady look. She had broadened a bit with middle age but still had a beautiful face. I got a cup of black coffee, mostly to have something to do with my hands. I guess I wasn't sure what I was going to face. She said "Thank you for meeting me. I've been visiting Sarah daily and I want to talk about her-and you." This did not exactly come as a surprise as the years have taught me that women will share aspects of their romantic relationship only with another woman friend.

She leaned forward and said "I have her permission to talk to you. How is she really doing?"

I said "The steroids and immunosuppressive drugs and plasmaphoresis have gotten us part way but not good enough. She can talk but is limited, and is not enough for her to go back to work. I'm going to ask Weston to take another look."

She said "That's pretty much what I thought. Suppose you get her better, what then?'

She leaned back in the chair. I knew where this was going but wanted her to spell it out.

So I asked "Meaning? "

She said "You know how she feels about you?"

I said "I've had a few hints."

She asked "What about you?"

I said "Pretty much the same."

She asked "So, happily ever after?"

I said "It's not that straight forward."

She folded her arms and asked "Why not?"

I said "Look, she's an attractive woman with a good job in an area with men as her coworkers. She can't lack for boyfriends. She told me about one and you mentioned the guy she met at church. She ended both of those for what for her were religious reasons. She is divorced but in the eyes of the Church still married. And in her eyes, I think."

She came back to the Church after a long bad time and now the only thing holding her together other than her friends and family, is her faith."

She seemed to relax a bit and asked "How long has it been for you? Maybe three, four years? What's your wife doing? Ever hear from her?"

I said "She's teaching back East. She calls from time to time."

She asked "She going with anybody?"

I said "How would I know? But given her religious beliefs, I doubt it."

She asked "Are you sure?"

I said "No but I haven't been contacted by lawyers yet."

Finally a smile.

She asked, "If she divorced you, would you remarry?"

I said, "Probably not."

She folded her arms and leaned back.

She asked, "For God's sake, why not? You don't do well alone."

I said, "Well, it's partly inertia, after living alone for a while, adjusting to another person might be tricky. Then there's the old religious echo. Look, this is not about me but about her and me and her beliefs and mine or in my case lack of belief."

She said "Why do you always wind up with the religious ones instead of a nice hedonist like me? Anyway, what holds you together?"

I said "Mostly collagen, just like you."

She laughed and said "You bastard. When I want a straight answer, I can't get it."

I said "Look, there is almost a generation between you and I and she and I. My family history is not encouraging. My father died at sixty-six, only a few years from where I am now. My mother died of Alzheimer's that probably began when she was in her seventies. I just go from day to day. If Sarah gets out of this place, it will still be day to day for both of us. As she told me 'Tomorrow is not promised.' We may be close friends; we may love one another deeply. We probably won't be lovers."

She said "I think I understand. But it's a damn shame to waste two bodies like that. Walk back to the locker room with me." We took our mugs to the busboy's station.

As we walked away, she took my hand and said "You know, when you came back from the East without your wife, I thought we might have had a chance. Yet you never made a move. Why not?"

I said "Well, I was trying to reestablish the practice, and after all those years together, I just could not figure out how to relate to another woman except in the course of the practice."

She asked "What about your needs, you know, for sex?"

I said, "It's a lot like, if you miss a few meals, pretty soon you don't notice the hunger."

She said, "Great, that's how people starve to death."

We reached the door to the women's locker room. She said, "Wait there a moment" and stepped inside. After a brief moment, she opened the door, took my hand and pulled me into the room. The place was empty. She said "Please don't hate me for this", and put her arms around me and held me tightly and kissed me deeply on the mouth. I responded as she knew I would, holding her and running my hands over her body. We clung to each other like drowning people and she shuddered for a moment then pushed me away and said "Now go, but don't forget me."

CHAPTER 16

By chance, Weston called the next morning, while I was seeing patients in the office. When I broke out to take the call, he said "Mac, I checked on your lady and I don't like what I'm seeing. Meet me in the lounge at noon; I'm giving a talk at eleven in the auditorium."

Lunches in the lounge vary from delicious to disgusting, mostly depending on the hospitals budget deficit. I toyed with the soup while Weston talked.

He said "We have got to do better or she will be ventilator dependent for life. At the end of this plasmaphoresis series, we have only sixty to sixty five percent of her pulmonary function back. And that's at her best. If we can keep her there, she could live without the vent during the day and get by with a positive pressure mask at night, but her life will be very restricted, maybe able to walk across the room, but no exercise or sports and probably never work again. And she panics as her respiratory strength fails, you can see the terror in her eyes. How was she when you saw her in the emergency room?"

I said, "She was terrified. Could barely speak. Almost no movement. She felt she was going to die and she was right. I've seen that look. She hasn't mentioned to me her experience that night. But I'm sure it's affected her. Well, what do you suggest?"

He said, "Let's push the steroids to one point five milligrams per kilo and push the cyclosporine dose as well. Then give her a course of immune globulin."

I asked, "Anything else?"

He took a moment before saying, "Yeah, talk to her about what we do if this is as good as we can get."

I asked, "Did you explore this at all with her?"

He said, "No, that's your job, and besides she seems to have this connection to you, so you two will have to decide together. We may never need to explore that if the medications work."

I said, "Let's hope so. I'd rather not face that. But thanks for the review. Maybe I should buy lunch."

He replied, "No thanks. I looked at the soup. Hunger's better."

He picked up his bike helmet; put a clip on the cuff of his pants and left.

He was right about the soup.

I went back to the clinic to finish out the day and to prepare to talk with her about the therapy plan. Chronic progressive diseases change peoples' souls, some diminish, others become better, simpler, perhaps more holy. The ancients thought of illness as the intrusion of death into life, as a decline in vitality or capacity to participate in life and love and in community. Physicians think of disease as disordered biology, neglecting the person's awareness of his life and his perception of the limitations on life that disease causes. People don't care about the science; they just want to know what will this do to them and their family. I have watched some of my myasthenic patients and patients with ALS deal with the disease impact on their life and learned that I could not predict given what I knew of their religious and philosophic background, what they would do or decide about treatment or end of life issues. For Sarah, I needed to know what her disease meant to her.

She was in the midst of the last plasmaphoresis treatment, and was tired and sleeping fitfully. I tried not to awaken her, but she sensed my presence. She opened her eyes and motioned me over to the bedside. The technician was changing the fluid bags and did not appear to notice that she took my hand and held it. She was on the ventilator so her whiteboard and marker were close at hand. She wrote "Glad you came. Weston was here."

I said, "I know, we talked over lunch or whatever it was. Anyway, you have reached a plateau with this and both of us think a trial of immune globulin and higher doses of steroids and cyclosporine are worthwhile."

She wrote "OK" and paused. Then she wrote "And?"

"That depends on how you do. If we can get you near to coming off the ventilator, we would continue with the infusions."

She wrote "And?"

I asked, "I'm not sure what you're asking."

She wrote, "If it doesn't work, what?"

Slowly I said, "Then there are decisions."

She shook her head and then wrote, "No, not yet."

I asked, "Weston said that you panic when you get short of breath. Do you want to talk about the night in the emergency room?"

"No, not with this" She waved the marker. "Come back in the morning when I can really talk. But don't leave yet. Stay with me for a while."

She took my hand and we stayed together while the technician tended his machine. Other than the sounds of the pumps and the muffled sounds of the ward phones and voices, there was some peace. At length, she took up the whiteboard. She wrote "Do you ever ask why?" I replied "I gave up. God doesn't answer; at least I can't hear the answer."

She wrote, "Probably shouldn't ask but I need to."

I asked, "What answer do you get?"

She wrote, "None that help. But I need to know."

I said, "Ask Father Francis."

She shook her head again "No, I'll get the standard Church answer. Suffering is good. I know that answer. Don't trust it."

I asked, "Who then, your pastor?"

Quickly she wrote, "No, you."

Surprised, I asked "Why me?"

She looked at me and then wrote, "You know the Faith but don't believe or trust it. Also you care."

I said, "I have no idea where to start. I'm a physician not a theologian"

She wrote, "The book of Job, start there."

There was a break, with both of us lost in thought.

Then I asked, "Tell me what to do if Weston and I are not as successful as you want."

She wrote, "Not now. Just stay with me."

The technician had finished the plasmaphoresis run and disconnected her from the machine and wheeled it out of the room. She appeared to be asleep, so I bent over and kissed her and she smiled in her sleep.

I did not know whether she would want to talk in the morning, but I needed to follow up on Weston's observation. When I finished my morning hospital rounds, I went to her room and found her propped up in bed, washed, brushed and ready with the speaking valve in place, to receive visitors.

I greeted her with "Good morning Sarah, I note a positive lipstick sign, which we physicians associate with improvement."

She said 'What? A lady can't dress up for her friends or lovers?"

I said "Which am I?"

She said "Both I hope."

I said, "Me too. Do you feel up to talking?"

She said, "OK. About what?"

"I want to know what you remember about the night in the emergency room."

She said, "I have tried to forget that. Well, OK, I remember for a day or two before feeling weak and short of breath at work. When I got home from work that night, I had trouble getting out of the car, and was more short of breath. I asked my daughter to take me to the ER. We sat in the lobby for an hour before the triage nurse came by and by that time I couldn't stand. They put me on a gurney and drew some blood and got a chest X-ray. The ER doc came by and did a quick exam and left. I think they put on oxygen by nasal prongs but it didn't seem to help. I waited and waited and then they sent me for a CAT scan, and then back to the room. I was seeing double by then and and couldn't swallow saliva. I tried to ask my daughter to get someone but could only whisper and could barely move. I keep feeling like I was holding my breath and couldn't let go of it.

I remembered once when I was water skiing, I jumped the wake and fell and the driver was talking to my girlfriend and didn't check the mirror. The skis pulled me under and I tumbled under water and couldn't get free of the tow rope. I held my breath until I thought my lungs would burst. I tried to stay calm and work free of the rope but I was scared to death. I felt that same sort of panic in the ER. The more I tried to relax, the more I felt that I was dying, and when I struggled to breath I would fatigue and get more short of breath. The worst part was that I tried to pray and couldn't. I was so scared. And then you came in and things started to happen. I don't remember much after that. But I know I don't ever want to feel like that again, the terror and helplessness. And the worst was I could not reach out to God."

"Now when you fatigue and get short of breath, do you still feel that terror?"

"Yes, I think it's worse even though I know I can recover back on the machine. It bothers me that when that happens, I have no control over my thoughts and feelings."

"Do you think that your prior depression has any bearing on this?"

"Yea, I couldn't control that spiral either. I was dead in my soul for a long time and only crawled back after a couple of years. How did you know about that?"

"Susan told me."

"She was one of my threads to sanity, a line of continuity from my childhood through the wasteland that was my marriage and the time after. I think God sent her even though she would deny it."

I noticed that she was pausing between phrases and seemed to be tiring. So I said

"Maybe I should call the nurse and get you back on the vent."

She said "Not yet. Give me a moment to rest. I have something else to say."

She took my hand and lay back with her eyes closed, breathing slowly. Several minutes passed quietly. Then she opened her eyes and said "When this is over, will we still be friends? I know that we can't be lovers or married but will you still be with me?"

"If you don't mind putting up with an old man, I've got time to make up. So, I'm with you till you tell me to get lost."

"Fat chance of that. Now give me a kiss and go get the nurse."

CHAPTER 17

I did as ordered and then wrote the orders for the immune globulin and cyclosporine. I had the nephrologists leave the plasmaphoresis catheters in place, a sort of belt and suspenders approach. The usual dosing of immune globulin for this purpose was four tenths of a gram per kilogram. In Sarah's case this was a dose of twenty six grams given in two divided doses for five days. I expected a scream from the pharmacy, because this represented about fifteen thousand dollars. Also, the stuff is in short supply as it is made from donated blood. I was not disappointed, as about fifteen minutes after the nurse faxed the order, my pager went off. It was the head of pharmacy, trying to be diplomatic.

"Doctor, are you sure you need this much IVIG?" she asked.

I replied "You should be glad the lady doesn't weigh very much. Besides, this is within the indications."

"Yes but it comes in ten gram units. Can we give her twenty grams?'

"No. To save you breaking and wasting a unit, give her 30 grams, in two doses. That would be five tenths of a gram per kilo. And I may need to repeat the course, depending on how she does."

"It will take a couple of days to get that much with the rationing, our neighbor across town has five units but the admin doesn't want us to call them."

"Well, I sure wouldn't want to upset the hospital politics. Just let me know when there is enough to start."

I was starting a call week, meaning the office schedule lightened up, and the pager and cell phone ruled. There were periods on call when little happened and during one of these periods, I began to consider this relationship, not so much in its ethical aspects, although those were important but to my mind pretty secure. I had other opinions, psychiatric counsel and chaperones in the form of nursing staff. No, it was more the moral and spiritual aspects that needed thought. She had asked me to stay on the case no matter what, and I had agreed. It was more than a little ironic, that I, who harbored doubt, had committed to a person of faith and was now wondering where each of us would end up. If she recovered, I would have a friend, at least, of my own faith, however shaky that might be. If she did not, I could not imagine how I would feel. I lose patients to disease frequently and don't usually take it as a personal or professional failure. Losing Sarah would be both.

As I've indicated, a lot of what I do involves determining brain function or the lack of it. Some of these patients are trauma victims; others are damaged as the result of illicit or prescribed drugs. Then there are the suicides that are occasionally original and inventive. Some throw themselves off parking ramps; others are single car collisions with bridge abutments. There are the usual pistols, ropes, belts and drugs. The latter often turn out unsuccessful as modern medicine can drag you back from the pit. This call week provided one of the most unusual methods. I was asked to evaluate a fellow who used his car to stab himself in the chest, a new version of falling on your sword. He had been arrested for some child pedophilia charge and was out on bail. The police had searched his house and carted off his guns and medications and slapped a global positioning device on his ankle. He could drive to work but nowhere else. His wife moved out and took the children. I guess he figured if he were convicted, which was likely, that prison would be an unpleasant experience, particularly if he ever wanted to take a shower. So he took a chef's knife, you know the one with the big blade and duct taped it to the center of the steering wheel and drove to work. Well, that is he drove about eighty miles an hour down the freeway and then stomped on the brake. Did I mention that he neglected to use his seat belt? He thus impaled himself.

Well, if you ever want to stab someone in the chest with a big blade knife, hold the blade horizontally, otherwise all you do is break ribs and divert the force of the blow. He managed to slice through his internal mammary artery and bled out a bit before the paramedics arrived. He did miss his heart, which was his target. Unfortunately, by the time the cardiovascular surgeons cracked his chest to remove the knife and repair the artery, he had been hypotensive long enough to be permanently comatose.

I ran the appropriate tests, including an EEG which was slow and unreactive, and a MRI that showed the death of most of his cerebral cortex. Now I had to get somebody to decide what to do. I first called his wife who by law had a right to decide. She listened to my description of his condition and probable future and said "Do whatever you want. I want nothing to do with that SOB.", and hung up.

Next, I called the detective whose card was taped to the chart and told him the story. He said "Sorry Doc, not my problem."

Next on my list was the lady from Child Protective Services who listened politely, and when I finished, there was a long silence and then she said, "I guess this means we can close this case. Thanks." Click

I still had to find somebody to decide. So I called the hospital attorney who told me that unless I could find a family member who would take responsibility, he would have to go to the court and get a guardian. Since the man was not convicted, he was not a ward of the state. Getting a guardian was going to take a long time and in the meantime, he would sit in ICU on a ventilator, at three thousand dollars a day, paid for ultimately by the insured patients of the hospital in the form of higher charges. We had already learned that his health insurance, which was poor to start, would not pay for care of injuries caused by a self- inflicted act. Since I had already wasted a couple of hours on this, I called the detective back to see if he could supply any further help. He said "Yeah, well, I think the wife mentioned a sister back East. Let me go through the file. I'll call you back." He called back five minutes later with the name that was different from the patient's which I took to mean that she was married. Figuring the time difference, she might be home, so the hospital operator placed the call. I have found this is more impressive and gets more cooperation than if I call cold. When I finally got her on the line, and confirmed that she was his sister and that there were no other siblings, I then explained the situation including the legal dilemma. Her first question was whether she would be responsible for the cost of his care. That being settled to her satisfaction, she then said "He was about ten years older than me and was always weird. He once tried to get me but I told Mom, and she told Dad who beat the shit out of him. He signed up for the army and I left home and haven't seen him since."

Ah, I thought, a glimmer of hope. Maybe I can sell him to the VA. I said "I didn't know he had been in the service." She said "He wasn't for long. Got a bad discharge for something." Oh, well.

Then she said "Look, if he can't wake up, you have my permission to terminate care. I won't shed any tears." At last. I had her repeat that to the nurse, then thanked her for her time.

I wrote the appropriate orders and then thought that even though he was a bad person, it's still a bit sad that the only response to his passing was a sigh of relief.

The pharmacy had managed in the next two days, to secure enough IVIG to begin treatment. When I saw her the next morning, she was sitting up in bed, reading, on the ventilator, whiteboard by her side. There was a half liter bottle of brown foamy liquid running into her IV line. I must have looked tired, because she wrote "Bad night love?"

I replied " The usual litany of human misery, headaches, drug reactions, strokes, back and neck pain, seizures, let's see , did I miss anything? I think they are having discount day at the emergency room."

She wrote "Why? Senior docs don't take call."

"Well, it helps when I want to go on vacation."

She wrote "Done that recently?"

I said "Well, no."

She wrote "Why?"

I said "No time"

She wrote quickly "Bull, you won't stop. Why?"

I had to think for a moment "Well, I don't really feel alive unless I'm working"

She shook her head and wrote "And so your life is practice? I see I have a lot of work to do."

I said, "Don't sign on. It has already driven one woman to despair."

She wrote "Too late. You don't get to vote. Now, about my question?"

I said, "Oh, Job. Well I'm part way there. Give me a day or two."

Well, Katie, I'm sure you read and discussed the Book of Job in your religion classes, but let me give you my take on after my experience with Sarah. Implied is the undercurrent that Satan wants to challenge God but doing so directly is a sure loser, so his next best move is to deride God's prize creation, man, a little below the angels but with free will and dominion over the earth. I had to read through Job several times and then tracked down a commentary that didn't help. Basically, I decided to write a summary of what I thought I had understood. This meant eliminating all the poetry.

Satan does an inspection tour of Earth and returns with a poor opinion of man and particularly Job. First off, Job is a righteous man, meaning faithful. God says so. Satan maintains that Job is righteous or faithful only because God favors him with wealth and family and protects him. It seems a wager develops, with God betting on Job. So to further the bet, God removes his protection, and Satan goes to work. First, a group of raiders steal Job's flocks and then some are killed by a natural disaster and then a natural disaster kills all his children. Job's reaction is to say God gives and God takes away, blessed be God. God says to Satan "See, I told you."

Satan says "Give me another shot at it. If his own life is threatened, he will do anything to save it." God says "OK, but you can't kill him." So Job gets a painful and disfiguring disease and is mocked and despised by the people he once ruled and cared for.

Job's wife, not pleased by his loss of station, tells him to curse God and die. For Job this would be spiritual suicide, so he refuses and instead bemoans the day he was born. He wishes he could hide in the land of the dead till God's wrath had passed and then God could call him back in favor. Thus God wins the bet and Satan vanishes from the story. Job is left alone, broke, despised and in pain and scratching his sores.

His solitude is broken by the arrival of three friends, presumably philosophers and rulers. They have one theme, that Job is being punished because he was sinful, since affliction was thought to be punishment for sin. They pursue this in a number of windy speeches, to which Job says, "I'm not sinful. And if I have minor faults, that's the way God made me, so why should he punish me for that which I'm not responsible." They can't prove that Job is a sinner so their response is that God can do whatever He chooses including punishing the innocent.

Job won't accept that God is unjust and still wants to know why he suffers. One speaker suggests that suffering is to make Job realize his sins and make him appeal to God for forgiveness. Job says "For what? What did I do that justifies this pain?" He can't demand of God an explanation. Job says if God appears in all his power and glory He would overwhelm me, I want to talk to Him as a man talks to his friend. Finally, Job gets his wish, but not quite like he wanted. Job has a private talk with God who appears in a whirlwind. God relates all the wonders of the universe that he controls, and tells him

"Look, I've got a lot of responsibilities, do you want to take over all this? Besides, who are you to question me, to accuse me in order to justify yourself?" Basically, God's answer is that Job should accept that God knows what He is doing. Job acknowledges that he has no right to question God. God has harsh words for Job's friends who accused God of injustice. For his friends, Job appeals to God in prayer and sacrifice. Because of his faith, God gives back to Job that which was taken from him. Persistence in faith is probably the point of the whole book.

Job never learns why he suffered, he just learns that God is just and compassionate and aware of evil. The problem of why the innocent suffer is never answered in the book of Job. This is the problem of evil. Either God is all-powerful, in charge of the good and the bad, or He is all good, but does not care or He cares but can't or won't help. It doesn't really help to assign the bad to another person, call him Satan or the devil because the same objection obtains. Is God in control of Satan or is he permitting evil?

But this is a problem only for those who believe in an all-powerful but loving God. If God does not exist or is arbitrary, there is no problem, at least for God. But in Job I could see some answers, more hinted at than expressed. The bad things that happened to Job came about through either nature or man. Does God control nature? Yes but God's justice is such that the world has to work the same for everybody. In a way, this evil is the absence of good, sickness the absence of health. The same immune system that protects us can attack us. Likewise the same processes that produce rain produce tornadoes. The legal term "Acts of God" is a just another way of saying the act was not due to human malevolence or negligence. I don't think that excludes miracles, but those are exceptional events, more like the intrusion of subatomic quantum mechanics with a different set of rules, into the visible world. God limits God's power for our benefit. Somehow the notion of God's justice is not too comforting when you're sick.

But what about the suffering caused by people? This is the issue that turns most thinkers off the concept of a loving God. The suffering and death of innocent children at the hand of adults, the mass genocides of our century prove there is darkness in the spirit of man, a love of savagery and brutality. I thought it interesting that in God's speech to Job in which He describes His control of nature and the animals, He never mentions man.

Here God took a chance. He could evolve another animal that would follow its genetic programming. Remember the Labradors we had that would cross their front legs when lying down, each generation with the right foreleg crossed over the left. Or He could make an animal that could reason, have passion and make decisions. To do this, He had to allow it to decide, in other words, free will. Freedom to love Him or itself. When a man chooses to put himself at the center of his world, he loses the capacity to love others. According to some Church thinkers including Augustine, man's decision to love himself led to corruption of nature so that it was hostile to man. I have no idea of what Paradise might have been like assuming the story is not a myth. Now however, nature is what it is, indifferent to man's desires .I don't know whether my dogs can imagine a world any different from what they experience, but I can. We have a sense of justice that isn't seemingly present in animals. Man is a chimera, a part of nature and somehow apart from it, part mud, part sky, drawn upward, and pulled back to earth. No wonder Milton had some angels thinking God had made a mistake. Like Job, I have to assume He knew what He was doing. I did not expect that this elderly altar boy would solve a problem that vexed theologians and provided fodder for atheist writers. Thinking this through had me eyeing the bottle of Irish whiskey in the cabinet, still with the seal intact. Maybe Houseman was right

'Malt does more that Milton can

To justify God's ways to man'

I had only partially answered Sarah's question why. She really wasn't asking who to blame, but what to do with pain and suffering. Suffering and death is part of this world and God permits it because to do otherwise contradicts His nature. The Church's answer is

that God suffered and died just as we do, and His death redeems
suffering. Without that intervention, the world becomes an alien
place for us. For the unbeliever, alienation is a fixture of existence. I
think Matthew Arnold saw this when he wrote

"The world ....

Hath really neither joy, nor love, nor light,

Nor certitude, nor peace, nor help for pain

And we are here as on a darkling plain

Swept with confused alarms of struggle and flight"

But that final agony very nearly cost Him his contact with the
Father. I think this was the final temptation, and it was what Sarah
was contemplating.

I'm fairly sure that the conclusions that I had come to were not
original and were probably better expressed by others including C.S.
Lewis. Now that my homework was done, I was prepared for Sarah
the next morning. Somehow, she managed to keep me off balance.
I'm not sure who had the bigger challenge.

CHAPTER 18

The next morning, she was up in the chair with the valve in place. She said "I have something to show you. Stay there." I was standing by the window, and she pushed herself out of the chair to a standing position and walked slowly toward me, a distance of maybe eight feet. She was slow and held on to the wall. When she reached me, her right knee started to buckle and I put my arm around her waist. She put one arm around my shoulder and rested the other on the windowsill. She managed to lock the knee and leaned against me.

She said "Vertical is better than horizontal. Is this going to cause you a problem?"

I replied "We can call it physical therapy."

She said "It is therapeutic, certainly. What do you think?"

I said "Best thing that's happened to me in some time."

And it was very nice to have something warm and affectionate next to me, especially since it did not have four legs, a tail, fur, long canine teeth and bad breath.

She said "We need to do this more often. But now, would you walk me back to the chair?"

Like a three-legged race we worked our way back to the chair, and she sat down and I sat on the bed next to her.

She asked "How long has it been now? A little over two months? Do you think the IVIG is helping?

I replied "So far. I'll be more certain after the next dose or two. But you do seem stronger.

She asked, "Is it time to hope?"

"Certainly, I couldn't function in this business without hope. Besides, once you're better, I plan to teach you to fly fish."

She laughed "You fish a lot? You actually have a life?"

I said "Mea culpa, I confess to one passion."

She said, "I hope you have more than one."

I replied "Well, you never know, new interests may arise."

Laughing, she said, "I can't believe you said that."

"You must have a corrupting influence on me."

She said, "Certainly on your sense of humor. Maybe we had better talk about your homework. Tell me what you got from Job."

I tried to summarize "Well, basically, God doesn't punish you for faults, and He is aware of a person's suffering."

She said, "True, but what happened to Job as a result of his suffering?"

I said, "He was depressed, wanted to die, he wondered why God was attacking him which He wasn't. He wanted to hide from God in death and thought that after death his spirit would see God. He could not believe that God was unjust or arbitrary. "

She asked "But what did the suffering do for Job? He was already righteous in his mind and in God's opinion. What did he learn?"

I said, "Well, there was a sense of pride in his righteousness, that he could demand of God an explanation for his suffering. His conversation with God made him change his mind."

She got to point very quickly "Is there an explanation for pain and suffering?"

I said somewhat slowly "The Church says that God allows the Devil to tempt us as a way of purifying us and God won't allow us to be tempted beyond our strength. I don't buy that. I don't buy that God tempts us or that the devil or whatever attacks us directly. There are bad people that cause others pain. I think pain, death and suffering are part of the world and the way we are, and can purify us or destroy us. I suppose the devil could take advantage of our weakness. What adds to our suffering is the memory of what we are and what we could be. Maybe suffering can push us out of a comfortable complacency and into greater dependence on God."

She asked, "I know God is aware of our suffering. Do you think He does nothing or is powerless to help?"

I said "I don't know what He does or does not do. I sense that relieving suffering is up to us as humans. Or at least we should not increase the amount of suffering and pain.

She asked, "How often in your years of practice have you seen pain and suffering improve a person?"

I said "Almost never. Most become self-centered and full of self-pity. They have problems reaching out just as Job did."

She looked at me for a moment and said, "I want you to promise me you won't let that happen to me."

I asked "How am I to do that?"

"Well, don't let me slip back into self-pitying depression or anger, keep reminding me to reach out to others. Do whatever you have to. Promise?"

I said "Yes, I promise. But you knew I would."

"I hoped you would. You hung in there so far."

"Part ethics and mostly affection."

"The affection part I like. Give me a kiss and get to your office. The physical therapist is starting with me this morning. One more question, for me and you, how do you reach out to a God that allows suffering but seemingly does nothing? I think I know but I need to know if you know. Now go."

I did as requested.

The next morning as I approached her room, she walked out wearing a hospital robe and the no-skid socks on the arm of a physical therapy aide. They went about twenty feet and tuned around and came back. As she passed me, she raised her hand for a high five. In the room, she remained standing as the aide left and then gave me a long hug.

She said "You know that the nurses know how we are with one another. They think we're cute."

I said "That's the last thing I expected to be called at this age."

I could feel her shaking with laughter as I held her.

She said "I think we're cute too."

With my arm around her waist, we walked back to her chair. She leaned back and closed her eyes for a minute and then said "I'm almost afraid to hope. This is the best I've been in two months, and I want to plan a life again. Do you see problems?"

I said "I'm never comfortable till the patient is out the door. And I get uneasy when things seem to go well. Still, I'm pleased that you're up walking and have more stamina. I'll finish this course of IVIG and then take a break and see how you do. You might need a second full course to get off the respirator for good. Thanksgiving is next week, and I'd like to have you out of the hospital before Christmas."

She asked "What are your plans for Thanksgiving?"

I said, "Well, my kids are out of town and have lives of their own, so other than taking a walk with the dogs, and catching up on my reading, not much else"

She said "Come here and spend the day with me. My kids will be here and I can tell you as a former employee here that the dietary department goes all out for those stuck here on a holiday. I'll guarantee that it will be better than tube feeds. I think you could smuggle in some Merlot, and we can pretend that this is the way it will be after."

"Lady, you got a date. Also, what would you like for Christmas?"

She replied "Just you and I together at Mass."

And hopefully thereafter.

In my past, Christmas was THE family holiday, and despite the religious differences, we managed to worship together, without debate. Coffee and presents after Mass, breakfast late, love and affection just as God would have it.

Chapter 19

My reverie was interrupted by a call from the emergency room. Bannister had a problem.

"Mac, I got the weirdest stroke here. It's a young Hispanic guy with a right hemi paresis, intact speech, and normal reflexes, no facial weakness and a normal CT and MRI. He doesn't have a headache or headache history. I did a LP and the fluid is normal. Come on down here and tell me what to do."

The ED was relatively quiet for once, one auto accident with several minor injuries, two chest pains rule out MI, and a lady in early labor. The patient was in room five, so I tracked down the nurse before looking at the imaging studies. She was one of the old hands, who somehow had managed to avoid the burnout and cynicism that pervaded the rest of the older nurses.

I asked her "Can you tell me any thing more than Bannister put in the chart?"

She replied "Well, his girlfriend is in there, and she has a bruise on her left cheek, so I think he hit her during a fight. Also, she had a ring on her left hand that isn't there now. When I brought up the possibility of abuse he started to cry and denied it. She said nothing, pretended that she didn't understand the question. I think he knows he f—ked up and wants her back."

I said "Not bad, Sherlock."

I did a quick review of the CT and MRI scans, both of which looked normal, though there was no radiology report back. It was time to check the flesh.

In room five, the patient was lying on a gurney, with an IV line in his left arm. The monitor above the gurney displayed his cardiogram, blood pressure and oxygen saturation, all of which were normal. He was a small, thin Hispanic man, no tattoos, whose eyes were red from crying. The girlfriend was sitting in the corner reading a novel whose cover showed a bare-chested man embracing a half-unclothed woman. I introduced myself and offered my right hand to shake hands. He raised his left hand. I asked him to raise his right arm or leg and he said, "I can't man."

I flexed his right arm and leg and noted the normal muscle tone. I held his right hand over his face and let it fall, and it fell sideways to his side. His reflexes were normal and he could smile on both sides. I put my hands under his heels and asked him to lift the right leg. There was no downward pressure on the left though he seemed to be trying. I started with a safety pin lightly touching him on the right chest and face and he gave no response till I reached the exact midline of his body. Human neuroanatomy is seldom so exact.

Well, Kathleen, as you might by now suspect, the patient's paralysis was not due to a stroke. Was it a conversion reaction, that is a sub-conscious conversion of stress into symptoms or was it a conscious act, which is malingering? Since no lawyer was involved, conversion seemed a better choice. I told the patient that I would talk to the ER physician and left the room to find Bannister. He was in the break room, stretched out on a couch, sipping a cola.

I said "It's a conversion reaction, call psychiatry."

He said "That's what I figured. But the shrinks will disappear when presented with something that looks like a stroke."

"So, admit him to the ward and start rehab."

He said, "No insurance. County won't pick up the bill for three months. Until then the hospital eats it. Fix it. Unconvert him, whatever."

"Why don't you just send him home?"

He said, "The Feds will be on my ass, EMTLA violation. Not stable, possible stroke. Just tell him it's all in his head."

I said, "Never works. You can't fix irrationality with rationality."

"So, do whatever you have to. Get him out of here."

I said, he said, "OK, do you have some nursing students or EMT students here?"

He replied, "Sure, also a med student. Why?"

I said, "No med students, they know too much. I need the nurslings for an audience. Also I need ten milligrams of Tensilon."

"Edrophonium? What for? He's not a myasthenic."

I said, "Better you shouldn't know."

He shook his head, saying, "OK, talk to the charge nurse and she will round up the students."

Pharmacy delivered a syringe of Tensilon through the tube system, and I met my flock of nurslings, and spoke to them outside the patient's room.

"Ladies, I'm going to use a drug on Mr. Gomez that has some significant cardiovascular effects. This is an experimental compound that you have never heard of, called neurotransmitter B. It may cause some bradycardia and sweating, so I will ask you to keep a close eye on the monitor, and to check the patient frequently. I'll discuss the pharmacology and physiology with you after the treatment. Don't ask any questions during the process. Understood?"

The chorus replied "Yes, sir."

We all entered the room much to the surprise of the patient and his girlfriend. I made my speech after positioning the students, one at the head of the bed, one at the foot to watch the monitor and the last to keep track of the patient's left radial pulse. I said "Mr. Gomez, I going to try an experimental drug to reverse your paralysis. The drug is neurotransmitter B, and it causes a chemical to build up in the body, which will increase the strength of the weak muscles. When the drug begins to work, you will feel some stomach cramps and your heart will slow down. This should not be dangerous for a young man. The nurses will keep a close watch on your vital signs. Is it OK to go ahead?"

Both he and the girlfriend said yes.

I turned up the IV rate to speed up the drug infusion and then injected two milligrams and waited a minute and then pushed in the remainder. In about three minutes, a brief painful expression crossed his face, and he passed gas. I said, "If you're feeling a cramp, that's good, it means the drug is working. Give it a minute, and then try to lift the right leg." He wiggled his toes and then slowly lifted the leg off the bed. I said, "Good, now try the arm." He slowly lifted the arm and held it over his head.

He said "Doctor, this great. How long will this work?"

I said "The cramps will end but the drug works for six to eight months." His girlfriend was beaming and the nursing students looked bewildered. I asked them to help him sit up on the edge of the bed and then went to get the head nurse so the IV could be discontinued and his discharge readied.

While the patient was getting dressed, I took my flock down the hall out of earshot of the room.

I said "Ladies, what you saw was a magic act. The patient suffered from a conversion reaction, an unconscious reaction to stress. Confronting him with this fact would fail, so I suggested to his subconscious a way to get better. The drug was edrophonium, which allows acetylcholine to build up, which caused the cramps, but which had nothing else to do with his improvement. Don't try this at home. The reason to have you all in there was to reinforce the suggestion or the magic if you will. Thanks for you patience."

I told Bannister that the patient could go home. He just shook his head.

Well, Kathleen, I won't recommend this ploy as you're working without a net. It takes only a minor lie to get the process moving. But if it fails, not only does the patient not get better but the doctor looks stupid.

Chapter 20

It was Wednesday before Thanksgiving, and the last bottle of IVIG was running in. Sarah was off the ventilator for up to six hours at a time. She was able to walk in the hall unassisted and once we walked to the outdoor courtyard, and sat until a sudden snow shower drove us inside. Back in her room, I fetched coffee from the unit kitchen, and we sat sipping it, content in each others company. She was able to swallow some liquids but still was on the tube feedings. For a while we had put aside any discussion of God and evil, just taking one day at a time, both of us a little afraid of the future. But it was also a good time as we both felt as though we had known each other for a long time. She asked me where I did most of my fishing. I replied that I mostly fished the river at a riverside park. She said, "I live near there. There is a path up from the river that I used to walk in the evening. I must have seen you there many times." I said, "Well, I doubt you would have recognized me as I'm not as suave and sophisticated when I'm on the water. I look more like some ungainly wading bird." That was followed by a peal of laughter that caused a nurses' aid to pop her head into the room to check on us.

I was not on call on Thanksgiving Day and rose early to give the boys their walk. The young yellow Lab pushed a jackrabbit out of the sage brush and gave him a bit of a run before coming back to me winded with two yards of tongue hanging out. The old Shepherd watched this with what seemed amusement, as if to say "why bother with something you can't catch?" A few flakes of snow were falling, and most of the aspens had shed their bright yellow leaves, and the hills had put on their winter colors of brown and gray. Heavy gray clouds were piling up behind the western mountains, suggesting a storm for the evening.

I met Sarah's family in her room and we adjourned to the floor family lounge for Thanksgiving dinner, which as promised was palatable though served on divided trays and no added salt. Sarah had most of her nutrition through the PEG tube, but tasted a bit of everything. I had brought in a bottle of Merlot, and some plastic crystal, which we managed to conceal from the nurses as they made their rounds. Sarah and I shared a glass, which surprised her kids, though her daughter seemed accepting of the situation. When I left, she gave me a kiss. No one seemed surprised.

That Friday I checked Sarah's respiratory function data after the last IVIG treatment. She had dropped only two percent from the previous values, which may have been random variation. I was unsure whether to have the plasmaphoresis catheters removed and rely on the IVIG only, or to leave them in for now. Unable to decide, I left them in. The rest of her lab work looked stable, though the cyclosporine was eroding her kidney function a bit.

When I went to check on her on Friday evening, she seemed somewhat subdued, though glad to see me. I asked "Are you feeling OK?"

She replied "Yeah, but I need to talk to you or Father Francis. One of the people in my Bible study learned I was sick and came to see me yesterday after dinner. She implied in so many words, that I was ill because as a divorced woman, I had dated a married man."

I said, "But you broke it off is what Susan told me."

She nodded, "Yeah, but I'm doing the same thing with you. I'm a serial adulterer."

I said, "Well, I guess that makes me one too. Hey, let me order up a half ton of rock and we can stone each other. Is this crazy or what? I thought adultery required a bit more than a hug and kiss, if you know what I mean. I'm glad she's not my friend. Besides, I thought you implied this person was Christian. Karma is an Eastern concept. Your thoughts and deeds come back to you strictly proportioned. Catholics believe Christ broke that link. Besides, if being good was easy, who would need a Savior?"

She said "Intention counts."

I said "True. But what is intended? Friendship, affection? Look, we both know the rules and we both play by them. I don't think loving someone is a sin, unless."

"Unless what?"

"Unless boundaries are crossed. Look, men love their wives, differently from their children, differently again from their friends. Friends can love one another, look after their needs, be united in spirit with them and never have any more contact than a hug or a handshake. What is that saying "Friends help you move, real friends help you move bodies"?

She said, "But I want more than friendship, ultimately."

I said, "So do I, but that's where we start."

She said, "Sometimes I wish I wasn't raised in the Church, that I could do what my heart told me and not worry about the consequences. Remember the hawks?"

I nodded and said. "Sure, but they have rules too, built into their DNA, just as we do. We are primates, maybe advanced, with reasoning, opposable thumbs and language, but still with the needs of our hairy cousins, for contact, comfort, and another primate to attach to. We didn't leave any of that behind, and if we can't get it we die or turn into murderers."

She said, "You've been alone for a while, what did you become?"

I said, "Maybe a bit of both."

She asked, "Are you happy that way?"

"No."

She motioned me over to sit on the bed, as I sat down, she pulled me back to lie beside her and put her arms around me. I put my arm around her shoulders and pulled her close. It was a long moment before she said "You know, this is better, I don't feel like murdering any one. How about you?"

I said, "Have a pulse and am peaceful."

She said, "Good. Same time tomorrow. Now it's almost time for my therapy." And she kissed me.

CHAPTER 21

After the start of the intravenous immune globulin therapy, time seemed to slow. I think the urgency of finding a diagnosis and effective therapy had lessened and we began to enjoy each other's company. My "official" rounds were made in the morning, with the chart and Jean the charge nurse. Jean and I reviewed the lab data and vital signs and made whatever adjustments seemed necessary. Jean and Sarah had developed a friendship that went beyond the usual empathy that good nurses feel for their charges. Their mutual contact point was Susan who had worked on the neuro ward some time ago. At break time, the three of them would be huddled like conspirators. Noon and evening were social rounds. We would talk about most any thing: poetry, baseball, fishing, cooking, and Bible passages, but not much about our past lives, or about the unforeseen future. Mostly we kept in physical contact, holding hands, hugging or just touching. There was a sense of joy and desperation as if our souls lost contact, we might never regain it. In the evening she would fall asleep holding my hand. I would watch her sleep, her breathing regulated by the ventilator.

A couple of days after the last IVIG dose, I noted that she was tiring slightly more and spending more time on the ventilator.

I checked her pulmonary function studies and found that her numbers had dropped below sixty percent of normal. As the week progressed, I noticed that she seemed to be tiring faster, going onto the ventilator sooner. Her pulmonary function data showed a steady decline. When I brought up the subject, she said "I knew I was slipping, but I didn't want this to end. Jean noticed it first. I asked her not to say anything. I was afraid. I was afraid if I get better, we will go back to being relative strangers."

I said "Ethically, I probably crossed the line some time ago, allowing the friendship to develop. But when you're better, you can fire me and I'll arrange for continuing care by one of my colleagues. And then we can be as close as friends as we can manage."

She said "Deal. Now come and kiss me."

It was clear that another course of treatment was necessary. The pharmacy told me it would take a week to round up the volume needed. They went ahead with the order with only a minimum of screaming. Pharmacy called me two days later and said they had enough IVIG to start the second course. I told them to start as soon as possible.

CHAPTER 22

The call came the following morning when I was on rounds in ICU. The pager gave the ward number and the code for stat response. As I reached for the phone, the overhead page announced "Code Blue station 32 room---." And it was Sarah's room.

In an emergency, waiting for an elevator can be an eternity, but I caught the code team from ER and tagged along. At Sarah's room, the crash cart was open at the door, and Jean had fitted an Ambu bag to Sarah's trach, and was trying to ventilate her. Jean trained horses and raised hunting dogs and had a grip that could crack walnuts. Still she was straining and using both hands to force air into the patient. Sarah's heart rate was one hundred twenty with a systolic blood pressure of eighty and her oxygen saturation was eighty percent despite one hundred percent oxygen fed into the Ambu bag. Sarah's face and arms were covered with hives and her eyes were swollen shut. The culprit was on the IV pole, a partially empty bottle of IVIG, the first dose of her second course of treatment. The code team physician drew the same conclusion as I did, anaphylactic shock, and gave her IM epinephrine. An infusion of antihistamine, theophylline and high dose steroids was started and after about five minutes, the nurse was able to ventilate her with one hand. The code team set up the ventilator and hooked Sarah to it and set up the machine parameters. I called for a bed in ICU and called the nephrologists to set up a plasmaphoresis for that morning to clear out the offending antigen.

Allergic reactions to IVIG are not common, but her response clearly eliminated that form of therapy. I would have to rely on plasmaphoresis and immunosupression, which so far had not been enough to get her off the ventilator permanently. I kept her in ICU, sedated till the stiffness in the lungs had subsided and the facial swelling had diminished so that she could open her eyes and then moved her back to the ward.

She was awake, in bed on the ventilator, when I saw her that morning. She had her whiteboard and marker, and wrote "Hi, what the hell happened?"

I replied "You had an anaphylactic reaction to some component of the IVIG. What do you remember?"

"Itching all over, and then wheezing, short of breath... Then panic, again. It was worse than that time in the ER."

"I'm sorry, I didn't see this coming."

"What can't see the future? What am I paying for?"

I said "I don't think you're getting your money's worth with me."

"Not so fast. You and I are in this together, right?"

"Yes."

She wrote "OK, now what?"

"IVIG is out. The next reaction would be fatal. I'll ask the nephrologists to speed up the plasmaphoresis. The steroid doses and cyclosporine are as far as I would want to go. I'll ask Weston for any other ideas."

"OK, can you guess the odds of getting off the blower?"

"Considering the recent experience, not too good."

"Hope you're wrong."

"It has happened that I've been wrong. But if I can't get you off the respirator, what then?"

"Don't know, haven't faced that yet. Can I count on you, no matter what?"

"Yes, partly because I don't want your decisions to be influenced by my presence or absence, but also I want to spend as much time with you as we have. That's my selfish motive."

She motioned me over to the bed. I slipped under the respirator tubing and IV lines and held her. She buried her face against my chest and seemed to be crying, though she could make no sound. I asked "Are these good tears or bad?"

She just shook her head and went on crying. After a minute or two, she picked up the whiteboard and marker and wrote "Talk to Weston, and give me some time."

I put in a call to Weston that morning and when he called back, related what had happened with the second course of IVIG. He thought for a moment then said "We got a problem. The plasmaphoresis will remove the immune complexes due to the IVIG sensitivity, but probably can't reach the intracellular problem. Plus the cyclosporine may leave her open to tumor development at some point. And she will be respirator dependent. Not a good fate for a young woman. It's theoretically possible that a bone marrow transplant, essentially giving her a new immune system might work. I can't recall any reports or studies of that procedure for sero-negative myasthenia. There would be a huge risk. The chemotherapy and whole body radiation to totally eradicate her native bone marrow would be arduous. Finding a compatible bone marrow donor would be a problem, but she has siblings some of whom might be close enough to work, if they volunteered. Then after the transplant, she would have to be in isolation for weeks to months while she grows more bone marrow and immune cells, and despite our best efforts, she might catch one of the nasty, resistant bugs that live here. With MRSA or VRE and a non-existent immune system plus weak lungs, she might die a slow and agonizing death. Mind you, I'm not recommending this, but you need to discuss the possibility with her. Maybe you should talk to one of the oncologists about the risks and benefits. Given her background, she may already have thought about this and discarded it. There is something else. You need to think about what you will do if she decides not to live her life on a ventilator. I can't conceive of taking a conscious, vent dependent patient off respirator support. That's like putting a plastic bag over their head. With the usual comfort care orders, she might struggle to breathe for hours to days. Are you too close to discuss this with her?"

I said, "Too close, I don't know. She has said that she cannot go through another episode of near suffocation."

Weston continued, "Then it would be palliative sedation or euthanasia, whichever term you prefer. Are you prepared for that?"

I said, "No, not yet. And my preference doesn't matter. It's the same thing."

He said, "The medical board or the DA might have their own definition."

I said, "So, it still doesn't matter."

He said, "I thought you were Catholic."

I said, "I am, or I was. The operative phrase is was. I know the moral reasoning, but disconnected from the religious background, there is not much sense to reasoning about intention and double effect, if the act has no moral significance or eternal consequences.

He asked, "What does your heart tell you? It counts as much as reason."

I said, "I won't let anyone die by slow suffocation, especially her. She would despair of God and even though I might not believe, she only has her faith."

He shrugged, "Do what you need to do. I've got no other ideas. But make sure the chart covers your ass."

"Thanks for all your help. Please stay on the case for now."

He said, "OK. Good luck." The line went dead.

CHAPTER 23

I pushed ahead with the plasmaphoresis, and readjusted her medications. After a week with five out of seven days on plasmaphoresis, she seemed no stronger. In fact she seemed to be moving less and was less interested in therapy. She seemed glad to see me and wanted to be held. She wrote comments on ward life and personalities and Jean and Susan spent afternoons with her. But I could not get a clue to her thinking. Someone had brought her a large yellow legal pad on which she wrote pages when I was not present. I asked Jean about this but she said that it was a private matter.

I finally got the courage to ask her thoughts about the situation, and she handed me a letter on the legal pad the text of which I include below as I cannot paraphrase her words adequately.

Dear Dr. B,

I wrote this to explain my decision before you brought up the question. The failure of the immune treatment made this more urgent but I suspected from the start that I might not survive. I now see that that my best medical outcome will be transfer to a ventilator capable nursing home in the southern part of the state away from family, friends and you. There I will die slowly of neglect, loneliness and despair. This shall not be.

My life has taught me that prolonged suffering will destroy me and my faith. Oh, I know we are taught that God will provide grace sufficient to get through any ordeal. Still, we pray to be delivered from evil. This is also a grace.

I had hope for a while and you kept that hope alive. Now I know there is no hope. I have discussed my decision with my family and they understand and agree. So now I need you more than ever. I don't want to die. I want to live, be with you, see my grandchildren and grow old with you. But this will not be. I want to stop the treatments and the respirator support. But I cannot go through what I went through in the emergency room, which now seems so long ago. As you love me, make my death as painless as possible. Do we not pray for the grace of a peaceful death? Be my grace. Do what you must to protect yourself, but do not fail me.

I would ask one more favor. I may be somewhat distant as I approach the end. Stay with me no matter what. Don't abandon me to myself. Talk to me, hold me, kiss me, anything.

Lastly, I know we will be together again. I will wait for you.
Love,

Sarah

I read the letter slowly, and realized she had the most realistic assessment of her outcome. I looked up from the letter to see her anxious expression. I said "I hate it but I will do what you want. When?"
She wrote "Maybe a week, before Christmas."
I said "OK, what else can I do?"
She wrote "Priest, Sacraments. Stay close."

I said "There are some things I need to learn from you before."
She wrote "What?"

"Simply, how you deal with hopelessness. For a number of years, it seems all I do is help people die. I know that I can help them live with a degenerative disease, but they and I know any victory is temporary. Whatever happened to 'I have come that they may have life and have it more abundantly'? There's a line in the Hound of Heaven that goes

'Whether it be man's heart or life it be which yields
Thee harvest, must Thy harvest fields
Be dunged with rotten death?'

I don't blame God. Most of the misery comes from us or from the world. It's just that we know we will die and yet struggle against that knowledge all our lives. Other primates don't seem to know or maybe care. It's like we are an alien species, yet part of the world."

She wrote "True, between angels and beasts we are. Still, I need to think how to answer. Stay with me and hold me for a bit."

I held her and she seemed to drop off to sleep. I quietly slipped out to write orders for the ethics committee to meet and review her request. I also called my psychiatric consultant to evaluate her for competency. I had no doubt about her right to decide, or her ability to decide, but in our legal climate, I wanted everything on paper.

CHAPTER 24

Out of professional courtesy, I called Marlowe personally to describe the situation and the reason for consultation, which was the need for an emotional assessment and competency determination. His first question was "So how many patients are we talking about?"

I replied "Just one ...for now."

He asked "Why do you worry about competency?"

I said "Well, we had a lot of religious discussions before she made her decision."

He said "So? What's that got to do with competency?"

I said "I just thought you ought to know."

He said 'I'll explore that aspect. But I doubt it will have any bearing on her competency. Her emotional state and how much you influenced her are more critical."

I said "She may have influenced me more than the other way. It's hard to describe the relationship. The term friendship would cover it but that could mean anything from a drinking buddy to an almost lover. Still, the discussion could have influenced her decision. We talked about the value or not of suffering. Her big fear is that prolonged respiratory support would destroy her faith again."

He asked "Some people manage with nearly full time vent support. Why can't she?"

I said "Ask her."

He said "OK, now was the relationship such that she would not want to burden you, for example, if you two married?"

I replied "Marriage was not a possibility for either of us."

Then he asked "Living together?"

Reply "No."

He said "OK, I'm beginning to get the picture. She cannot not believe and you don't believe but act like you do. Lovely. We need to talk when this is over. For you, it's not the end but the end of the beginning. I'll see her tomorrow. I presume you're convening the ethics committee and would want me present?"

I said "Yes and yes."

I knew I would have to talk to the oncologist despite our prior encounter. His name was Mackenzie and he had been at the University as long as I had been in town. If any specialty has a more hopeless outlook than neurology, it has to be oncology. The really common tumors, lung, breast, melanoma, pancreas and brain generally have poor and frequently painful outcomes. I knew I would need his expertise and hope to avoid his nihilistic philosophy, which while understandable, was a little too close to mine. When I called his university office, I got the usual phone menu. I checked the office Rolodex card that gave his extension and that got me through to the departmental secretary who took the patient's name room number and the reason for the consult. She promised he would call me back. He called me back late the next day. I told him what his former colleague Weston had suggested. Relating the whole story took several minutes. He was silent for a moment, then said "Weston's gone round the bend. Spent too much time in the woods. But I'll look into it. I suppose you will want me at the ethics committee again?"

I said, "Yes, if you would."

He said "Tell me about this woman. Is she able to sustain what might be a highly risky treatment with probably life-long problems? If not, there may be no point in my getting involved."

I replied "She has a year of medical school and a Masters in nutrition." I was about to continue when he interrupted me.

"I didn't ask about her intellect. I asked about her psychological resilience. How tough is she?"

I've never been sure what "tough" means when applied to a woman. She bore two children, survived a disaster of a marriage and recovered from depression. I mentioned all this, and then added "She has a strong religious faith."

He said "Is that supposed to mean something? Never mind. I'll look into it and get back to you."

I didn't get a chance to say thanks.

Marlowe reported back to me the next afternoon. "She is a little sad at the way things have gone and is having some anticipatory grief, but is perfectly in command of her faculties. I put a note in the chart."

I asked "What about her religious belief? Did that drive her decision?"

He said "If her belief system doesn't affect her thinking and decisions, it's irrelevant. But if having a belief in God and an afterlife is abnormal, then a majority of humans are abnormal, which makes no sense. No, she is perfectly rational."

I said "I'd like to ask if our religious discussions about suffering led to her decision."

He said "Look, our communication was limited and my brief was simply to determine her mental state. I know you are concerned that you may have influenced her. I can't judge that. Given that there was more emotional involvement than docs usually have with patients, there probably was influence, but good or bad, I don't know."

I said "Answer me this, would it have been different if she had had another neurologist as you suggested?"

He took a moment and then said "No. The therapy you and Weston carried out as far as I know was conventional. Whether an experimental procedure such as stem cell or bone marrow transplant would have been helpful is not for me to say. Try oncology. She did mention the spiritual vacuum she felt when unable to breathe and avoiding that sense is critical for her. She also felt that long-term respirator support was unacceptable but did not specify the reasons. I didn't ask either. But there was a reason she wanted you to stay on the case and it does involve whatever relationship you two developed. She trusts you to do the right thing. Will you?"

I said, "A lot depends on what the Ethics Committee decides."

Bluntly he said, "No, y'all are evading. They will most likely decide that she can decide. You probably know why she decided the way she did. I'm a Baptist; I can't follow all the Catholic reasoning. You have to decide if you can carry it through. Take the logic to the death."

I said, "Thanks, I was fairly sure she was competent. And I do understand her reasons. As for carrying through, I'll wait till I hear from oncology before I commit. He said, "And when this is over, we should talk."

Did I mention that he tended to be blunt?

Mackenzie called later that afternoon. He said, "Have you got a few minutes?"

I said, "Sure. I've got a hole in the schedule."

He said, "Good. I talked briefly with the patient, reviewed the chart, and ran a Pub Med search. Here's what I came up with. There are no reports of stem cell therapy in sero-negative myasthenia. In animal models of myasthenia, there have been some attempts to reverse the disease with stem cells. There are two models: one using autologus stem cells from her own bone marrow, the other using allogenic stem cells from a matched donor. The autologus cell plan would have the best long-term outcome since she would not need life-long immuno-supression once her bone marrow regenerates after whole-body radiation and chemotherapy with high dose cyclophosphamide and reinfusion of her cultured stem cells. There is one small problem. Auto-immune diseases are stem cell diseases, meaning that self derived stem cells contain the genetic material to make the same auto-antibody that is causing disease now. So all animal experimental attempts to treat auto-immune diseases using autologus stem cells have failed. That brings me to allogenic stem cell therapy. There is the usual radiation/chemotherapy regimen and then the life-long immune suppression which may lead to tumor development. But here there are two problems and both depend on the donor.

If the donor is a close genetic match, say brother or sister, the stem cells may have the genetic capacity to develop the same auto-immune problems that autologus stem cells have. If the match is not close, then there is the risk, which is substantial, of graft versus host disease shortly after transplant.

All in all, given that there are no human studies and the problems with stem cell transplants that we do know about, I would not recommend pursuing this line. It is futile.

At the meeting tomorrow, I'll present this option, with a negative recommendation. I have briefly discussed this with the patient and she agrees with me. But I have concerns about her reasons for her decision, which she would not discuss. In my view, the reasons may be critical in our decision."

I said, "That's a very concise review, and I appreciate your work. I had tentatively come to the same conclusion without the background that you have. As to her reasons, that may need to be discussed tomorrow but they may not be relevant to the committee's decision since her competence and autonomy will be the principle factors in the committee's consideration."

He replied "That's true but her reasons may have a lot to say about her competence. Even psychotics have logical reasons for what they do but the reasons are not what the sane world accepts."

I said "I've talked with Marlowe and he thinks she is competent but perhaps a discussion of the patient's background and philosophy may be helpful."

He said, "All right, tomorrow will be interesting."

The Ethics committee met at 7:30 AM in an old section of the hospital that was closed for remodeling. Again, the meeting room was a recycled utility room complete with sink but slightly larger than the room used for the previous meeting. The linoleum was worn and faded and there was the musty, faintly urine smell common to old facilities. There was a table and four chairs, one of which had a yellow stain and seemed to have been exiled here after its unfortunate clinical duty. Davidson was the chairman and was paging through the chart as we gathered. Other than the chairman, the attendees were in no particular order, Jean, Dr. Weston, Dr. Marlowe, Father Francis, Dr. Mackenzie and me. As people entered, positions were adjusted so that there was a maximum of distance between people, just as the passengers of an elevator readjust with the gain or loss at each floor. Jean and I stood as did Dr. Weston.

Davidson opened the meeting by summarizing Sarah's case, and mentioning that he was a consultant but would vote, rather than recuse himself. He then set out the decisions to be reached: was she competent to make any decision and whether the decision she made was in fact, appropriate and rational, meaning informed. He asked Dr. Marlowe to establish her mental status. He quickly stated that she was not significantly depressed, that her thoughts were coherent and she knew the consequences of her decision. Dr. Weston reviewed the therapeutic maneuvers and said that with conventional therapy, basically plasmaphoresis and immunosuppressant drugs she would be ventilator dependent most of the time and would require nearly total care. He also added that stem cell therapy had been considered. Davidson said to put that off for a minute and asked Jean to speak. Jean said she had talked to the care coordinator and that the only facility capable of her care was in the southern part of the state four hundred miles from her family. She also added that Sarah did not want to burden her children with her care at home. I noticed that Jean's voice was a bit tremulous and that she was wiping her eyes with a tissue as she spoke.

Davidson nodded to Mackenzie who, as promised related his research and said that with the data available he would not recommend stem cell therapy and in any event, no insurance would cover the procedure. He started to ask why she decided as she did, but Davidson said not yet. Next up was Father Francis and the question to him was the moral hazard to her in stopping respirator support. All present knew her "religious preference" as the hospital face sheet designates ones faith. He said in the eyes of the Church, that respirator support for life is an extraordinary measure, which she can refuse without moral hazard. Then he said softly "I will vote but as her priest for now I can not reveal her reasons. It is enough to believe that her moral hazard would be worsened by trying to live on respiratory support for the rest of her life."

Davidson said "I think we have enough data to judge her ability to make a decision. All in favor of certifying her right to decide for herself?"

The vote was unanimous.

None of this was unexpected. Now we had to determine if she made her decision in an informed fashion. That she understood the physical consequences of staying on the respiratory support or not was an issue, at least to my mind. Dr. MacKenzie spoke up first addressing me "When you asked me to look into the experimental therapy, you mentioned that there were religious issues. I recall you said she has a strong religious faith. I don't understand why that should lead one to die when quite a few respiratory failure patients manage a respirator and lead useful and fulfilling lives. I've seen it with my lung cancer patients and I'm sure you have with your motor neuron disease patients.

He sat back as if waiting for an argument.

I said, "Yes, it's true some respiratory failure patients choose long-term ventilator support and others do not. I'm sure you have cancer patients who refuse or stop chemotherapy even when you think it would be helpful. I, for one, have never been able to predict who will accept support and who will not. It may be that my lack of understanding is due to the fact that as physicians, we see the patient as disordered biology that can more or less be put right. I know that the patient doesn't know or really care about the biology. They need to know how the illness or therapy will affect their lives or the lives of their family. I'm sure you have seen cancer patients who tolerate difficult therapy just to get to a point in their life that has importance, such as a daughter's wedding or a grandchild's graduation, and then stop treatment and accept death. I think informed consent means more to the patient than knowing the effects of treatment or the consequences of refusal. The patient has to estimate how the treatment will affect the things vital to his life including his faith and his family. All of us have dealt with patients whose faith prohibits acceptance of blood transfusions, even when their live is endangered. I may not agree with their decision, but they make an informed decision based on concepts vital to their spiritual life.

To return to this patient, she has told me, over the three months, how essential to her is her spiritual life and how past experiences have shown her it's fragility. I only nominally share her faith, yet I understand why she made her decision. Personally, I wish it were otherwise."

Davidson said, "Thank you." Then he said, "I move we accept her decision as informed. All in favor?" The vote was three to one in favor. Mackenzie left first, followed by Fr. Francis who patted me on the shoulder as he left. Jean and I stayed behind as Davidson wrote in the chart the committee's decision. As he wrote, he paused and looked up and said, "You'll write the usual comfort care orders?"

I said, "Yes, comfort care."

He looked at me a moment, nodded and went back to writing.

Jean took my arm as we left the room. She asked, "When?"

I replied "When she's ready."

She said, "I want to be there."

"Ok." I said, "I'll let you know in case you're off that day."

Walking back to the ward, I realized that although we had affirmed her autonomy, it was a hollow victory. I thought of another line from 'The Hound of Heaven'

"The pulp so bitter, how shall taste the rind."

The ethics committee wasted no time in certifying her right to stop treatment based on the psychiatric opinion. All that remained was to pick a date and time. When I saw her the next day, I was reluctant to bring up the subject. She spared me by writing "I'm not quite ready yet. Must finish." And pointed to the yellow legal pad. Then "It's for me and you. Kiss me." I did and held her for a long moment. I didn't particularly care what the staff thought. Time was running out. She wrote "The letter is both an explanation and a prayer. Keep it and think of me."

She handed me the letter the next day and wrote "Tomorrow." And took my hand and held it. I kissed her for the last time.

Father Francis gave her Communion the next morning and we set up the portable ECG monitor. The family gathered and we had an IV line running. I pushed ten milligrams of morphine and five of diazepam and disconnected the respirator. She seemed relaxed and soundlessly said "I love you" to each family member. Her daughter held one hand, and I held the other, and felt her pulse at the radial artery. For a moment she seemed at peace and then her heart rate picked up and she started the struggle. I pushed more morphine and diazepam and she relaxed and her eyes closed. Then she opened her eyes, looked at me and said "I love you." She closed her eyes and her breathing attempts stopped. In a few minutes her heart rate slowed then stopped. The monitor alarm went off, and the nurse silenced it. She was gone.

She died two weeks before Christmas. The family sent me a card thanking me for my care of her. I didn't attend the funeral.

I'm enclosing the text of her note to me without paraphrasing.

Dear Dr. B,

I have finalized my affairs with my family. The children will share the house and my pension will go to them and to any grandchildren. Except for one thing I am ready. I would have loved to give myself to you but failing that I would like to share one episode in my life as my legacy to you.

You know I left the Church for a long time and wandered in despair supported by the prayers of my friends and family. I could not reach out to God then, as you cannot now. Probably not by chance, I went to a Good Friday service. I'm sure you remember as an altar boy, that there is no Mass on Good Friday, but the liturgy is moving. I remember singing the Negro spiritual "Were you there when they crucified my Lord" Mostly though; it's the dramatic reading of the Passion. And one part especially- the next to last words of Jesus "Father why have you forsaken me?"

He had come to Jerusalem as a super hero, hailed as a Messiah, and in less than a week, this good innocent man was betrayed, tried and convicted in a kangaroo court for political expediency, beaten and then nailed to a tree to die in agony. The massive adoring crowds were gone and most of his friends had deserted.

Every night He had gone out alone to pray to his Father and received comfort and guidance. Not this day. There would be no Voice from a cloud, no cure and no miracle. God the Father was silent. Jesus was fully human at this moment, dying a failure without hope. I know he had his faith in the Father but as you said, as a human, doubt and faith walk hand in hand.

I understood something twelve years of Catholic education had failed to impart. That to reach the lost, hopeless ones, as I was and you are, He had to become like them. And by his faith, rise to offer hope to the hopeless.

I hope this helps you. In my love, it's all I have left to give.

Love always,

Sarah

CHAPTER 25

About a week later, early in the morning, I stopped in the doctor's lounge for a cup of coffee and a look at the newspaper. Marlowe sat down opposite me. He said "Y'all look terrible. Are you as bad as you look?"

I said "It hasn't been a good week."

He said "It's not over is it?"

I said "No, it's not."

He said "How long do you intend to keep poking at the sore?"

"When does it heal?"

He said "Takes a while, and there's always a scar."

There was silence for a moment, and then he said "We need to talk this through. Come to my office late today, say four o'clock.

I asked, "will it change things?'

He said "For her? No. For you, maybe."

"OK, I'll be there."

His office was in the oldest part of the hospital, built in the late 1800's. Most of what were hospital rooms were converted to offices for those in the hospital bureaucracy whose rank did not entitle them to a place in the new, gleaming glass enclosed tower.

He was standing in the hallway, talking to a resident, and waved to his office saying "Be right there."

The office had the gray-green paint that must have been standard décor back then. I've seen it in every Veteran's hospital that I worked in or trained in. One window looked out on the parking lot. A battered gray metal desk, two hospital chairs and a small bookcase nearly filled the small room. Off in a corner was a small bathroom with a shower stall but no curtain, a toilet and a sink. Benign neglect by housekeeping was evident. The walls had the usual multiple certificates, licenses, and diplomas that every physician accumulates. The only personal touch was a framed group photograph of young men in short white coats and 70's style haircuts and clothes, labeled University of Alabama-Birmingham Class of 1975.

He walked in and shut the door. I suddenly felt nervous, I guess, at the prospect of talking about myself with another professional. I said "Hey, you got a private bathroom."

He said "Yeah, one step above a privy."

I said "I guess you would know."

He said "OK, enough of the Southern jokes."

I said "Sorry. I guess you miss the jasmine and magnolia."

He said "Yeah, a bit. Pull up a chair. No notes, no recordings. Medical privacy is a joke."

"Thanks."

He said "So tell me how this relationship developed."

I said "It was a routine doctor-patient relationship until I asked Father Francis to see her. That started a conversation about the Faith that led to friendship if not love."

He interrupted "The Faith and Catholicism- that's another culture. I had an English professor tell me you couldn't understand Shakespeare's plays without some knowledge of the Catholic faith. There are still things in Hamlet that I can't follow. But if you don't believe, how did you get drawn into the conversation? Did she seduce you?"

I said "Did I want to be seduced? Doesn't seduction imply some sexual attraction? No matter how attractive, a woman with an endotracheal tube and Foley catheter isn't much of a turn on. No, I doubted my doubt and it was a relief to discuss things with someone who understood. As you said, it's a different culture, or was when I was part of it. It's difficult for a non-Catholic to appreciate the solitary nature of the Mass. There is none of the fellowship that is prominent in Protestant congregations, or so my wife used to tell me. Also, I guess I was feeling somewhat socially isolated."

He asked "Speaking of that, how much do you think your marital problems were a factor in your involvement?"

I said "How can I be objective about that? Sure, patients and dogs don't satisfy the need for understanding."

He asked "Suppose she was not in respiratory failure, imagine she was a woman patient in your office for, Oh say for a migraine?"

I said "Not likely. The religious factor would not have been present. We treat disease as an abstraction, cut out pity, close our hearts. The religious discussion opened up a vein of poverty of soul in me. In that sense, I was seduced. I've been in the business long enough to recognize sexually seductive women, and they always put me on my guard. I picked up nothing. "

He said "OK, let's move on. Tell me about your emotional state as this case progressed."

I said "Well, at the start, I can't recall any particular emotion. It was a busy call week. I recognized that she was an attractive woman and that may have made me more empathic than usual, which isn't much. It was only after the diagnosis was made and treatment started that an emotional relationship developed. And then it was none of the crazy teen-age, obsessive infatuation that I've heard people experience with a new romantic interest. It was more like meeting an old friend for coffee, that kind of comfort feeling. Even when we were both suspicious that success seemed unlikely, neither wanted the feeling to end. But of course, it did."

He then said "Tell me about the religious discussions."

"We talked about faith and doubt and the value, if any, of suffering. I now wonder if that particular conversation led her to refuse further respirator support. I was pretty negative about it, mostly seeing the world of misery, suffering and death. I know there are some people and some religious who find some value in suffering, claiming it develops appreciation for life and gives us an opportunity to love and care. I can't see it myself. I really don't understand the Church's notion that human suffering makes up for whatever was lacking in Christ's suffering."

He said "You didn't have the influence you think you did. She had come to her own conclusion based on her life experiences. All you did was validate what she knew. Every patient with a chronic disease has issues of control. It's not egoism but a means of preserving personality in the face of overwhelming illness."

I asked "Do you suppose that's why she refused to let me off the case?"

He said "There's that and she knew that you would do whatever was needed without abandoning her. I guess you know that the ICU nurses refer to you as the Angel of Death.'

"I know. They can predict what I say in every family conference. But that's the nature of hospital neurology practice. Estimate as best I can the patient's chance of survival or recovery, then talk to the family and try to find out their wishes or what the patient would have wanted and act accordingly."

He asked "Did you ever have to do this with a fully conscious patient?"

"Not quite this way, with a young, totally aware person. Nor with the others was there the emotional attachment. Still, none of that should matter morally."

He asked "Speaking of that, how do you feel about the end?"

I asked to clarify "What aspect-moral, legal or emotional?"

He said "Start with the emotional part first."

"Right now, it's like emotional wack-a-mole. I'm never sure what I'm going to feel from moment to moment. I can never tell what will trigger a mood. If I see a woman on a respirator, hear a discussion about suffering or see some hawks riding the thermals and off I go on some emotional tangent. How long does this last?"

He said "Intense grief reactions last a couple of months. You just have to walk your way through it. Something will always remain, but you will be able to function. Drugs and alcohol don't help."

Well, I wasn't going to do that anyway. He took a moment to formulate his next question.

"What about the morality? As a Catholic or ex, that might still be an issue for you."

I said "You mean once a Catholic always a Catholic even if you're not? Whose morality, hers or mine?"

"Go with hers, if you can."

I said "In a sense, she was a martyr, because she refused to let an evil disease destroy her faith."

"So you don't think she committed suicide by doctor?"

He got to me with that one. I was immediately angry, which was better than feeling nothing. I said "That's ridiculous. She had every right legally and morally to refuse extraordinary treatment which long-term ventilator support meant to her. And in this state, her doctors have to abide by her decision, or if they have moral qualms, find someone who will."

He said "Since you carried out her wishes, I assume you moral uncertainty was nil."

"You would be wrong. Even though I may not be very Catholic now, I haven't forgotten the principle of double effect. The notion is that the use of medication to relieve suffering during death from respiratory failure is acceptable, even though the doctor knows that the dosages of medication may hasten death. Morally, everything lies in intention."

He asked "And what was your intention?"

I said "Let me put it this way. When I'm fishing and land a trout that I want to keep, I hit it in the head, rather than let it thrash around on the shore or in the landing net."

"What about legally, do you think there will be a problem?"

I said "Look, doctors, nurses and combat soldiers are up close and personal with death all the time. For the rest, including lawyers, it's an abstraction, until it happens to them. There's no way to convey the reality, so there's no point in trying. I'll just have to wait and see what happens."

He said "Here's a possible therapeutic question. Would you do it again?"

He was right. This took some thought. I said "In a similar clinical situation, probably. But in a personal sense, it's unlikely that an identical situation will arise. As you told me early in this case, it's better to practice without personal involvement. Go back to dealing with disease as an abstraction, a collection of symptoms and signs in a biologic organism. I don't like that solution. Do you have any other ideas?"

He said "You haven't taken any time off since she was admitted. The best, non-pharmacologic therapy I can recommend is for you to get away from here for a while. Take a break, go back east, go visit your family, anything but stay here where the environment triggers memories. Take at least a week, more if you can manage."

I said "That's a good idea. My colleagues could cover the practice for a week or so, and I can get someone to house-sit with the old dog. The sooner, the better. How much do I owe you for the therapy?"

He said "What therapy? This conversation never happened. See you around."

CHAPTER 26

Three days later, after a flurry of phone calls and some begging, I loaded up the young Lab, Buster, and headed out with only a vague idea of a destination. Mostly northwest, through the low passes in the Sierra, through national forest land. The dog rode shotgun and was a good listener but had not much to say. I mostly planned to stay in national forest camp sites, developed or otherwise and sleep in the back of the truck, a practice I would not recommend after the dog had his dinner. Well, Kate, I'm sure you remember our camping trips as not exactly luxurious which explains why your mother hated them. Catholic camping was her term, you had to suffer.

This started an extensive conversation with my self. Buster was the straight man. To be seen alone talking to yourself invites curiosity, people think you're off your meds too long, especially if you don't have a cell phone in hand. Although the whole trip was an exercise in mourning, the first day was the worst. The usual sense of excitement and freedom associated with the start of a trip was replaced with an emotional deadness. Buster usually has his head out the window getting high on the scent rush. This day, after a few sniffs and a sneeze, he laid his head on my leg as we drove northwest. The first camp was along Hat Creek and the roadside campsite was primitive but empty and Buster could roam at will. But after his usual toilet function and bush check, he hung around the back of the truck after dinner.

I pulled out the Bible and reviewed the verse that began this story. I understood why she had refused to let me off the case. She assumed, based on my care of her mother that I was professional, would not give up and would manage the case without emotional wear and tear. She probably also knew, from having worked in the hospital until recently, that I would not let someone die in agony. I could accept all that. Doctors get used to death. It's like having a neighbor live next door or down the street that you see from time to time.

Dusk was falling as I finished reading Psalm 139 again. This was the Psalm to which her faith referred. I mean her final faith position. Her beginnings were like mine- conventional Catholic. The coyotes were beginning their evening chorus and Buster did not appreciate the musical interlude. It was time to button up the back of the truck and turn off the small flashlight that I was reading by. As I drifted off to sleep listening to Buster's snores and the coyotes singing, I was struck by the thought that if her life was determined in advance, then mine was too. She could have just as easily come under the care of one of my less religiously sensitive colleagues.

At dawn the next morning, Buster got restless. I popped open the back and dropped the tailgate. Cold morning air flushed out the doggy smell along with the dog. I sat on the tailgate and fired up the camp stove for coffee and oatmeal. Buster did his business and wandered around checking bushes and surprised a breakfasting bunny. Since there was no particular destination, we took our time packing up and then headed northwest again. We were heading toward the Cascade Range and as I looked up far in the distance, I could just make out Mount Shasta with its east face glacier shining in the sunlight. Having to look up to see the top of the mountain, made me recall a conversation that Sarah and I had one evening when therapy was going well.

We were sitting in a ward lounge whose windows faced the western mountains and we watched the sun go down behind the mountains. The sky faded from bright to orange, then to red then to purple and then to black. I remarked that I had loved to watch this sequence when at sea, but this was different. She said it was different because you have to look up away from the earth to the sky. People still think heaven or God is there. They set up altars on high places. Jesus went up on the mountains to pray at night. Then she quoted the opening verses of Psalm 121 "I lift up my eyes to the mountains. Where will my help come to me?"

Then she said "You were an altar boy in the days of the Latin mass. Wasn't the altar raised above the congregation? Do you still remember the Latin?" As I recalled the conversation, I remembered when finding my father's course syllabus, I also found some old photos in an album. One was of him and me together. I was in white shorts, white shirt and long white socks, a First Communion picture. A few pages further, I was standing alone in black cassock and white surplice, now an altar boy. I guess I was maybe nine in the photos, an age when boys and girls look alike except for the hair, all thin arms and legs and soprano voices.

Kathleen, some pictures of you at that age are similar to the old ones of me. It was lucky for you that you wound up better looking. The Mass in your experience was in English and the acolytes are both boys and girls. The congregation gives the responses and the priest faces the people. In the bad old days, the altar boys gave the responses in Latin.

Ah, yes, Latin. "Introibo ad altare Dei. Ad Deum qui laetificat juventutum meam"
"I will go unto the altar of God. To God who gives joy to my youth."

Joy? I suppose so. An only child is the center of his parents' world. I was a good student and that pleased them. I remember long summer vacations with my cousins. Even the storms of early adolescence were tolerable. My parents shielded me from the stress and anxiety they must have felt as my father's career faltered. The shield failed during a period when we lived with relatives. The crowding and the financial stress came to a head one evening in a crowded dining room when my uncle's wife attacked my father with a knife. Even though she was a known schizophrenic and later died in an institution, it was still a memorable event and we moved again. We lived in an apartment near a convent school. I served Mass there every weekday with a Franciscan friar for over a year. Always faithful- then.

By noon, Buster and I had passed Mt. Shasta and pushed on into Oregon. I had a vague notion to see Crater Lake but needed to find a camp site before dark, which comes early this time of year. About three o'clock, I spotted a logging road and turned off and took it for about a mile where there was a small clearing. From the clearing there was a small game trial leading uphill to an outcrop of black volcanic rock. I climbed up to a relatively flat spot to stand on and look out over the valley below. Buster had had enough of my thinking out loud and found bushes and trees more interesting than my memories. From my perch, I could see a number of large, dark birds circling over one area. Clearly these were not hawks but buzzards or vultures. Some substantial creature was down and dying or already dead and they were waiting their turn for ground dwelling predators to finish.

The sun was already low in the west. I called Buster back and headed back down to the truck. I gave him his supper then fixed something for myself. Some ground squirrels were disputing our squatting in their territory, so they got the scraps in payment for rent. Sitting on the tailgate, as the sun went down, I went over the memories that the Latin phrases evoked. For the most part, that ten year old boy was still here, somewhere. But I don't know if he could hear again "I have loved, O Lord, the beauty of thy house and the place where your glory dwells." The vultures that I had seen earlier were roosting in the trees surrounding the clearing and muttering to themselves as they settled in. I buttoned up the truck wondering if they knew something.

By first light, the birds had left for breakfast, making a great racket and dropping branches and pine needles in the process. I let Buster out and made coffee and studied the map. It looked possible to drive around Crater Lake and then push over the Cascade Range and push onto the north coast. I felt the need to get to a place with an interface, a boundary where some decision seemed to await. Since it was early and mid-week, traffic was light and the park was almost deserted except for some hardy souls. The radio had predicted snow and a few flakes were drifting into the lower elevations. The ranger handed me a map and waved me through after a glance at the truck and passenger. A bit more snow fell as we wound our way up to the rim road. At one point we pulled over to get a better view of the crystal blue surface a thousand feet below. Bands of snow drifted across the lake like veils and the pines were swathed in white. Pulling further along the rim, I saw the vast pumice fields left when the volcano exploded to form the caldera. The fields have been there for four or five millennia, and still have little growth, though now the snow was drifting across the grey surface. I know there are places in our own state where atomic testing has sterilized the earth. My geologist friends tell me that no matter how deep they go there is no life, not even bacteria.

The contrast between the snow shrouded crystalline lake and the barrenness of the pumice fields made me a little sad, and I wanted to push on to the coast. The rangers had closed some of the higher portions of the rim road, so we retraced our route back to the turn off for the pass over the Cascades. This entailed a climb of a little over one thousand feet to reach the pass and despite the plow trucks, the snow was drifting across the road. I pulled over to the side, got out and locked up the front hubs and back in the truck, put it in four wheel drive. We were able to plow through the drifted snow and reached the summit and started down. Then the fun began. On the windward side of the mountain, there was ice under the snow and at the first turn, the back end of the truck broke loose and started to slide to the guard rail. The truck's four wheel drive system, which was helpful getting up the hill, was now causing the anti-lock brake system to be less effective. I had grown up driving on roads like this back East and the drill came back to me; before the curve, gentle brake, double clutch, downshift, low power around the curve, up shift for the straight, repeat. Brake too hard or miss the shift and we would be sliding again. I looked out over the edge to the drop below and wondered if this trip was such a good idea after all. Buster sensed my concern and looked over at me several times as if to say "Boss, are you sure you know what you're doing?"

After a half hour of gritting my teeth and sweating, I realized I should be praying that we didn't fall off the mountain. But then, prayer requires a belief that God exists and can or would respond. Shortly after that thought, the road leveled out in a stretch of national forest. Signs indicated a campground a mile further down the road. That seemed like a good place to sit out the storm. At this lower elevation there was a mixture of light snow and mist. The campsite was secluded and there was the dead stillness that snow and mist bring. I let Buster roam around while I fixed his supper and mine. Buster came back to the sound of his food dish and shook off just beneath me adding to the mist and fog. The back window of the truck cap kept the rain off me as I sat on the tailgate watching the mist drift through the pines. Except for the hissing of the stove, all was quiet. I realized that I hadn't spoken to a human being, except for store clerks and gas station attendants, for several days. So far that was OK as my interior dialogue had a ways to run.

I went back to the cab of the truck, folded the seat forward and got out the still unopened bottle of Irish whiskey, broke the seal and poured a double shot into my coffee cup. I don't like to drink alone but Buster prefers water. The chill was penetrating and dusk was falling. I lit the gas lantern more for heat than light. Buster hopped into the back of the truck and settled in for the night. I sipped the whiskey, giving thanks for the Irish monks who developed it as well as other civilizing influences.

Monks. The altar boys would kneel on the lowest step of the altar on either side of the priest and bowing down would recite the Confiteor in Latin.

"Confiteor Deo omnipotenti, beatae Mariae semper Virgini, beato Michaeli Archangelo, beato Joanni Baptistae, sanctis Apostolis Petro et Paulo, omnibus Sanctis, et tibi Pater: quia peccavi nimis cogitatione verbo, et opera: mea culpa, mea culpa, mea maxima culpa."

"I confess to Almighty God, to Blessed Mary ever Virgin, to Blessed Micheal the Archangel, to Blessed John the Baptist, to the Holy Apostles Peter and Paul, to all the angels and saints , and to you Father, that I have sinned exceedingly in thought, word, deed. Through my fault, through my fault through my most grievous fault."

What does a ten year old boy have to confess? Dirty thoughts? Inappropriate pleasure in certain body parts? The Church was big on guilt back then. Examine your conscience; surely there must be something bad. Nothing comes to mind? Bring up some old stuff; you have got to have something to follow "Forgive me Father, for I have sinned." I, like a lot of people, got stuck there for years. There was no way out if you stuck with the rules, avoid this, and don't think that. Getting unstuck required living through adulthood, if not growing up.

It was now dark and cold and the mist was freezing. The whiskey had done its work, inducing relaxation and sleep. I turned out the lantern, buttoned up the trick, patted Buster on the head and zipped up the sleeping bag. As I drifted off, I had the thought that most of the failures in my life were my own fault. Mea culpa, Mea culpa, mea maxima culpa. Through my most grievous fault. Amen

We awakened to a translucent light. At first, I thought that our breath had frosted the windows inside. But a quick wipe revealed the frost to be outside. I pushed open the back window and Buster and I pushed our heads out to discover a totally white world. The tulle fog had frosted everything, truck, tree trunks, pine needles and the ground. Such beauty does not last. The sun was warming the metal of the truck and the tree trunks were shedding their innocence. I thought it would be better to wait till the frost and black ice vanished into the air. We had a leisurely breakfast, kibbles for the dog and some oatmeal and black coffee for me. I pulled out the map and plotted our course to the coast. It looked like we could make the Oregon coast by nightfall and find a place with a real bed and a shower. Buster smelled much like he always does but I was getting a little rank and the beard looked like I had slept under a bridge for some time, which was close to the truth.

Once the roads looked wet rather than shiny, we set out. I took up the thought of last night, my failures, and my fault. Let's start with family. I can recall getting to one of your basketball games and one cross-country meet. Your sister fared worse. I got to some of her karate matches but not her track events. I sometimes wonder where the heck did these girl athletes come from. I read once, that military fathers, especially Navy fathers, are more like a metaphysical concept, known and admired but seldom seen.

Your mother's story is more complicated. She had the responsibility for the house, you kids, elderly family and not much support other than financial. And then there were the career changes and moves not all entirely voluntary. I will need to come back to that but you need to understand why your mother did what she did. What you probably can see, now as an adult and medical student, was your mother's need for intellectual achievement. Before you were born, when I was a resident, she did her Master's degree with a thesis on cardiac electrophysiology during endotracheal suctioning. Her major professor was an RN who supported herself through her PhD program in physiology by working as a ward nurse. She was your mother's major professor, thesis advisor, mentor and role model. She was also a fellow graduate student with me during my graduate studies.

That need never left her despite having to take on the roles of mother, care giver and household economist. Even though it took eleven years to finally settle in one place, she never gave up the dream. And you know the rest. When you and your sister were in high school, your mother at age forty- seven began graduate school in molecular physiology. Degree in hand, the climb up the academic ladder began, with the result that our paths diverged. Fellowships on the East coast, another on the West coast, I tried to keep up but could not leave clinical practice for good. So "Two roads diverged in a yellow wood" as Frost said. Two late middle-aged people abandoned love and laughter for loneliness and transient achievement which is a current summary of the present situation. But that was not the first. There are relatives that I lost touch with, friendships that I did not maintain and colleagues whose motives I doubted. Mea culpa.

As Buster and I made our way on the back roads into the basin between the Cascades and the Coastal Range, I returned to my thoughts of the night. How is it possible to have a sense of sin, a feeling of guilt when I'm uncertain about love of God? Is this some sort of religious hangover? It is possible to build a system of ethics based on human dignity without reference to a deity. But an ethical violation in such a system is more like getting a traffic ticket and doesn't bring the feeling that sin does. All sin is turning away from God and thus turning away from the possibility of love. I had certainly turned away from love most of my adult life and when I didn't, it was for the wrong reasons. The effect on me and my capacity to believe and trust was significant. Sin brings its own punishment. Who needs a hell? Turning away from love brings a bit of death, a constriction of life.

We were now in the valley heading for the I-5 under pass to get to US 101 along the coast. Traffic was picking up in the towns and I needed to concentrate on driving. Talking to Buster was now out of the question and he turned his attention to the open passenger window. Past I-5 we hit 101 and went north. After an hour or so, I found what I was looking for, a no tell motel, not far from the beach with an open field for Buster's toilet. The elderly Indian gentleman behind the desk took my information card, looked at the truck and said "No dog in the room."

I said "Sure, no problem." He shook his head and handed me the key. Our charade being completed, I got back in the truck and drove to the farthest unit, parked, and opened the door. The unit was clean, threadbare and musty. Next to the bed was a coin slot for the "Magic Fingers" massage device on the bed. Although the sign on the parking lot said "Family Motel", the last time a whole family stayed here must have been in the Nixon administration. I let Buster out in the field to explore while I stared at the ocean. The northern Pacific is a much different ocean than the sunny Atlantic of summers at the Jersey shore. It's colder, darker, and more depressing, especially in the winter with snow and mist scudding across the waves.

When Buster had explored to his heart's content, I put him back in the truck and got out of the cold for a warm shower. After a trickle of rust, the shower head finally produced a miserly spray of lukewarm water enough to generate some lather. Dried off and in clean clothes and a jacket, Buster and I set off to find a fast food joint for dinner. He had dined on dry kibble but always appreciates French fries. I needed a break from the dehyrdrated camp meals which in my hands are several steps below MREs. Back at the motel, I took the flashlight and found the path to the beach behind the motel. Buster joined me after his exploration of the field. I found a washed up log that had been stranded where the dunes met the beach and sat there to stare at the surf. I had run as far west as I could go. Here the demons would have to be faced, but not tonight. Back at the truck, I got the dog's blanket and the bottle of whiskey, and then using the blanket as a drape, escorted Buster to his place beside the bed. I would have to have him out before first light, but was counting on the old desk man to sleep in. I poured a double shot into one of the motel glasses and lay back on the bed sipping the whiskey.

I could hear the sound of the surf through the thin walls. Matthew Arnold had heard the same sound and it caused him to mourn the loss of faith in the world. His conclusion that

"The world...

Hath neither joy, nor love, nor certitude, nor peace, nor help for pain...'

matches mine. But still, faith like the tide ebbs and flows and though for me, the tide was still out, the pounding on the shore signaled the possibility of comfort.

Just before first light, Buster became restless and his pacing woke me up. In my stupor, I first thought that the French fries had upset him. Then I heard the wind howling and shaking the thin walls. I dressed quickly and took the flashlight and went out to the trail to the beach. In the gray light of the false dawn, I could see the surf breaking on the beach, but the spray, low clouds and mist obscured the horizon. Sea and sky seemed blended together with no boundary or interface. The Biblical story of creation mentions that the Spirit of God hovered over the waters, but I sensed nothing. A particularly strong gust picked up loose sand and drove it into my face. I turned around to get my back to the wind and from where I stood; all I could see were three low mountains and the woods. The fog obscured the foothills and the town. Buster was anxious to get out of the wind and this seemed like a good time to get coffee and breakfast and let the squall pass.

After a leisurely breakfast, we returned to the beach for a walk and some exploration. The wind had died down but there was still a light mist on the water. The beach was littered with flotsam driven ashore by the wind and tide. We found small logs, glass fishing floats and dead creatures like fish and squid and of course, seaweed. Buster had a fine time running in and out of the surf, chasing gulls. He didn't seem to mind the cold water or the cold wind. I remember from my Navy days that an unprotected person in these waters would survive only twenty minutes or so. The hypothermia puts you to sleep and you drown. Not a bad way to go, strip down, swim out as far as you can and let go. I used to think that death was a binary event, zero or one. Now I'm not so sure. Maybe there are degrees of death, the more you drop out of the circle of life, the more nearly dead you are. I realized that after Sarah, I was pretty close, but I was not willing to let go yet.

I thought again of what Sarah has said and what she wanted for us or if not that, for me. Sarah was an interface, a person living in two worlds, God's and ours. She wanted to show me how to live that way and might have succeeded if she had lived. Her death closed the portal, at least for now. Buster, tired and wet from the surf, came over to where I had been sitting and lay down. We watched the waves together, break, then withdraw and return and break again, a cyclical process superimposed on the arrow of time. The beach changes with each wave and is never the same. Tennyson wrote
"But the tender grace of a day that is dead
Will never come back to me"
That brought me back to another of his works, Ulysses, who says
"Old age hath yet his honour and his toil.
Death closes all; but something ere the end,
Some work of noble note may yet be done,"

I understood at that moment, that I would go back and start over. A decision with a single degree of freedom, quit or go on. Another portal may open, or not. Maybe I just have to look in the right way to see it.

The storm had died away and it looked like a good time to get back on the road, this time without the dialogue. I planned to head north to the Snake River, then over to Yellowstone and back down to our region. No more guilt, no more thinking or breast beating, just pick up the load and carry it.

CHAPTER 27

The registered letter was waiting for me at the office. It was a formal notice from the medical board, charging "improprieties" in Sarah's care. There were no specifics, but they did want a written response and set a hearing date. Since they were vague as to the issues, my written response was basically a case summary. I noted by the agenda that they had been meeting for two days, but no witnesses were listed.

After I was sworn in, I noted that the stenographer's bin was already quite full. The direction of the inquiry quickly became clear as the following transcript potion indicates.

Board Counsel   "Doctor, we have heard testimony that you hugged this patient. Is that true?."

Doctor   "Yes"

Board Counsel   "We also heard that you kissed her. Is that true?"

Doctor   "Yes"

Board Counsel "Did you not think that contact was inappropriate?"

Doctor "Those contacts began after we became friends and were appropriate for a friendship."

Board Counsel "Were you sexually intimate?"

Doctor "No"

Board Counsel "I reviewed your curriculum vitae. It is impressive, multiple degrees, significant publications, and I note that you are married. Is that correct?"

Doctor "Yes"

Board Counsel "Are you and your wife living together?"

Doctor "No, she works out of state."

Board Counsel "Is there a formal separation?"

Doctor "Formal, I don't know. De facto, possibly"

Board Counsel "Are either of you contemplating divorce?"

Doctor "Neither of us."

Board Counsel   "I understand that you and the patient were of the same religious belief and had religious discussions. Is that true?"

Doctor   "Yes'

Board Counsel   "If she had lived, would you have continued the relationship?"

Doctor   "The friendship would have continued if I could find another neurologist to manage her myasthenia."

Board Counsel   "Why did you not sign off the case once this 'friendship' developed?"

Doctor   "I offered and she refused and this was before a personal relationship developed."

Board Counsel   "You could have withdrawn unilaterally, once the relationship developed and before your judgment became impaired by personal consideration."

Doctor   "I don't think my judgment was impaired. There was a monitoring second opinion. The patient was not non-compliant, and thus there was no valid reason to violate her autonomy, her right to the physician of her choice."

Board Counsel   "One last question on this topic. Did it not occur to you, a married man that this relationship amounted to infidelity?"

Doctor   "I saw the relationship as innocent. I don't deny, that in any relationship involving a man and a woman that sexual aspects exist, but they need not be primary. If anything, I might be guilty of emotional infidelity. Yet, any doctor's spouse has to share his or her partners life, energy and often, emotional commitment with patients."

Board Counsel "I'd like to move now, to the patient's final hours. The record shows that she refused further respirator support after various therapies failed. Her decision was ratified by the ethics committee. I understand that she picked a day for the event. Tell me how much influence your religious discussions had on her decision."

Doctor   "The psychiatric consultant told me later that she had reached the decision on her own."

Board Counsel "But you knew that later. Was it not unwise to engage in philosophical or theological discussions with a seriously ill patient who had an emotional attachment to you?"

Doctor   "No, it was not unwise. Understanding a patient's religious or cultural background is essential to being able to communicate with them or their family, and to formulate or adapt therapy to their needs. Also, unless some personal trust is present, patients will usually not discuss their religious beliefs for fear that they will be mocked or thought irrational."

Board Counsel   "Our consultants have told us that in such circumstances, a common practice is to order a terminal wean. Would you describe that process?"

Doctor   "In a patient with respiratory failure, the term weaning means that respirator support is reduced as the patient improves. It's an incremental process, based on accepted criteria of pulmonary function. On the other hand, if the patient can't be weaned and he or the family decline further support, the respirator is turned and the patient dies of respiratory failure, basically asphyxiation. Fortunately, most such patients are comatose but some are not. The term is a euphemism for letting the patient die. I don't like the term. It conceals from us the reality of our decisions."

Board Counsel   "What term do you prefer?"

Doctor   "I don't prefer any."

Board Counsel   "What is the practice for a conscious respiratory failure patient who declines further support?"

Doctor   "The practice involves palliative sedation."

Board Counsel   "How is that accomplished?"

Doctor   "The patient is sedated or rendered unconscious by drugs and the respirator is turned off."

Board Counsel   "What is the difference between palliative sedation and terminal sedation?"

Doctor   "Words"

Board Counsel "Words?'

Doctor   "Yes"

Board Counsel "All right. Now tell me how palliative sedation differs from euthanasia."

Doctor   "The principle difference is in intention. The second point of difference is in the choice of drugs and means of administration."

Board Counsel "How are we to know your intention?"

Doctor   "You don't. You can make it anything that suits your purpose. My intention was to make the patient's death painless."

Board Counsel "Putting that aside for the moment. Was not the dose of morphine and diazepam in total, sufficient to kill a patient, especially one with respiratory insufficiency?"

Doctor   "The dose of morphine that will seriously depress respiration is usually more than twice the dose that is safe in an adult. Ten milligrams of morphine intravenously is usually safe in an adult."

Board Counsel "But you gave that dose of morphine with a further respiratory depressant, diazepam and then repeated the dose of both. Didn't that prove to be fatal?"

| Doctor | "She was conscious but free of air hunger after the first dose, comfortable and able to say goodbye to her family. I only gave the second dose when she began to experience air hunger and fear." |

| Board Counsel | "You were aware that the second dose could prove fatal?" |

| Doctor | "Yes" |

| Board Counsel | "So explain to me why this final act was not euthanasia or physician assisted suicide." |

| Doctor | "Firstly, a patient who refuses respiratory support or other therapy and dies of their disease is not considered a suicide, assisted or otherwise. Euthanasia is deliberate killing. If I had wanted to cause her death, I would have given sixty millequivalents of potassium chloride intravenously, just as is done in the prison down the road." |

| Board Counsel | "I put this proposition to you. You persuaded this woman to refuse respiratory support because she was a therapeutic failure, a respiratory cripple who depended on you and would have been a burden." |

| Doctor | "What the f—k have you been smoking? That's gotta be the most outrageous statement that I've ever heard from an attorney in thirty years of practice. Maybe the Bar association ought to drug test their members before they renew their license." |

At which point, the chairman came out of his coma and said "Gentlemen, that's enough. This session is adjourned."

Given the hostility of the hearing, I could not foresee the outcome. They could issue a reprimand or a referral to the DA or let the matter drop. I let my attorney deal with the board. Our states laws are fairly specific as to how a physician must respond to a patient's desire to end treatment, either comply or find the lady another doctor. She had refused the latter several times and there was no point in revisiting the issue. There was the issue of personal involvement that I needed to work through. It's hard to avoid. Just in the course of taking a history we learn so much about a patient's life, concerns and failures. In many cases it's like looking in the mirror. There is an immediate understanding of how they felt, especially when our histories are the same in essence. I know that some physicians choose specialties that don't require close personal encounters or enable them to keep their distance. In my earlier life, I felt that way. Now the personal involvement is all that keeps my humanity intact.

So that is Sarah's story and mine. I did go to Christmas mass as she requested, alone. During the ceremony, a memory came rushing back. I remember one Christmas season, I was serving Midnight mass and the church was decorated and had two Christmas trees with a crèche beneath. It had been an unusually warm December and the church windows had been opened several times in the course of the decorating. Somehow two sparrows had taken up residence in the trees and were fluttering about during the service, much to the great amusement of the children present including the altar boys. The pastor was annoyed but there was little he could do. Toward the end of mass, it being warm, the ushers opened the windows again and at the final blessing both birds flew past the altar and out the window. I remembered the incident, when reading about an Old Norse view of life that we are like birds that enter the light and warmth of the house from the dark, enjoy a brief moment of light and grace and then are in the darkness once again.

When I was preparing my response to the board, I wrote to a friend from my research days, a woman physician with whom I had worked closely, and outlined both the facts and the my reactions to Sarah's death. Her reply was both brief and comforting. It was a fragment of a John Bell hymn
"Both end and beginning
Both message and sign
Both victor and victim
Both yours and divine"

CHAPTER 28

It was a few weeks after the hearing that my attorney called to say that the board had decided not to act on the complaint. His supposition was that they had gotten all the publicity they could out of the case. By then, we had one of those rare breaks that occur in the winter here, when there is a brief spell of spring-like weather, enough to fool the robins and tempt the fruit trees into suicidal blooming. I took the opportunity to sneak out of the office and head to the river, to the spot where we used to fish. It is near where Sarah used to walk. Remember the contests we had, first fish, biggest fish most fish? I took the fly rod along more for cover than to flail the water, so that passers-by would understand an old man staring at the water rushing by. A pair of mallards, drake and hen, were drifting in the water, presumably checking out nesting sites. The pair would lay and brood some eggs and hatch a flock of six to eight light brown ducklings each about the size of a hen's egg. Out of this little family, maybe two will grow big enough to leave their parents. Some will get swept away by the current, some will die of exposure or duck cholera, and some will become lunch for a coyote or feral cat. I wonder if the hen feels the loss, the breaking of a connection when one disappears. A French paleontologist, Teilhard de Chardin, once wrote that consciousness extended downward in the phylogenetic tree, so that even bacteria had some awareness even if very attenuated. I guess I'm not so concerned about what the hen does with her consciousness, but what we, meaning we physicians, do with ours.

The better we become at the intellectual and mechanical aspects of our profession, the more automatic become our responses to the patients needs. In one sense this makes us less able to respond to a patient's physical pain or to their suffering which is a more complex concept.

I've been in the business over thirty years and have seen two extremes of physician practice in response to a patient's pain and suffering. The first might be called denial, in that they ignore or minimize the patient's complaints. They prescribe fixed doses of pain meds regardless of the response and minimize the patient's pain by classifying the person as a drama queen or a drug seeker. This is infectious cynicism as it spreads to the doctor's colleagues and institutions and then finally to their families and friends. The other end of the empathy spectrum is those doctors whose solution to suffering and pain is death. I'm sure you have seen these around the wards. My favorite example is the intact old person with a slow but eventually fatal disorder who gets admitted for some other correctable problem and gets tagged with a no code order that winds up being interpreted as a no care order. Vital signs are neglected and routine labs limited and death results by benign neglect. Some of these doctors have an agenda, are proponents of euthanasia or assisted suicide. Most don't care enough to care about the outcome.

In between are the vast majority of physicians whose interactions with patients will depend on time pressure, sex and personality interplay. Almost all will be successful on both parts, the patient will have the problem identified and treated and will be grateful and the doctor will have the satisfaction of having done a good job. Both will part, each to his own world. And then, rarely, the doctor and the patient will remain united, bound together in the illness.

I wish I could tell you how to avoid cases like Sarah's. Maybe if you pick a specialty that has minimal clinical contact and build your personal relationships outside of medicine, you might do well. Maybe anesthesia, you know, meet the patient before surgery, put him/her to sleep, wake them up, say goodbye and send the bill. But if you pick a specialty that involves continuing care, you will eventually have to walk with your patient into the darkness. You will have to find your own way back to the light. I have no further advice. Give your mother a call and think of me kindly some time.

Love,
Dad.

GLOSSARY

Acetylcholine	A chemical transmitter between nerve and muscle
Acetylcholine esterase	Enzyme that breaks down acetylcholine
Allosteric enzymes	Enzymes regulated by compounds that attach to it
Ambu bag	A football shaped rubber bellows like device fitted with a one-way valve for ventilation of a patient
Anaphylaxis	An acute, explosive reaction on a previously sensitized person
Atropine	A drug that blocks the action of acetylcholine on the gut and heart
Bicarb	Bicarbonate of soda -used to reverse acidosis
Botulism	A bacterial toxin in spoiled foods that causes paralysis

Bradycardia	Heart rate less than sixty beats per minute
Brainstem	Back portion of the brain above the spinal cord, that controls life sustaining functions
Code gray	A hospital code to request security personnel
Conjunctiva	The white portion of the eyeball
CPR	Cardio-pulmonary resuscitation
CT	Computed tomography-X-ray technique that displays body parts in thin section-used to detect intracranial bleeding
Cyclosporin	Drug used for immune suppression and for prevention of rejection of transplanted organs
Cytoxan	(Cyclophosamide)-potent drug used for cancer chemotherapy
Diazepam	(Valium)-a tranquilizing drug
Diffusion scan	An MRI technique measuring the movement of water molecules in a tissue
Dilantin®	A commonly used anticonvulsant drug
Dilaudid	Hydromorphone-a potent opiate drug
Dopamine	An intravenously administered drug used to increase blood pressure
ECG	Electrocardiogram

ED	Emergency department or room
Edrophonium	Tensilon
Electrolyte	Ions such as sodium, potassium, chloride found in blood plasma
EMG	Measurement and recording of the electrical activity of nerves and muscles
Endotracheal tube	A soft rubber tube inserted into the trachea assuring airway protection
Ergotamine	Drug that causes contraction of smooth muscle in blood vessels and uterus
Glascow Coma Scale	A numeric scale for measuring level of consciousness
Guillian-Barre	A disease that attacks motor nerves and causes Paralysis
Heparin	A drug that prevents blood clotting
Herceptin®	Trade name for trastuzmab-a manufactured antibody used in the treatment of breast cancer
Hydromorphone	An opiate-Dilaudid
Hypomania	Part of the spectrum of bipolar disorder-increased but organized thought and activity
ICU	Intensive Care Unit
Laryngoscope	Instrument inserted into the throat that opens the airway and facilitates insertion of endotracheal tube

Lidocaine	A local anesthetic
Lorazepam	(Ativan®)-a tranquilizing drug
LP	Lumbar puncture-spinal tap to obtain spinal fluid
Medulla	Posterior portion of the brainstem containing centers that control blood pressure and breathing
Midazolam	(Versed®)-rapidly acting tranquilizing drug used for anesthesia during short surgical procedures
Midbrain	Uppermost portion of the brainstem containing Centers for maintainence of consciousness and for controlling eye movements
Morphine	A potent opiate
MRI	An imaging system using magnetic fields that visualizes soft tissues
MRSA	Methicillen resistant staphylococcus aureus-one of the so-called super germs
Myasthenia gravis	A disease that blocks the nerve impulses to skeletal muscle causing paralysis
NG tube	A tube passed through the nose to the stomach
NIH	National Institutes of Health-a federal agency

Opthalmoscope	A device for viewing the interior of the eye
Osteoporosis	Decreased calcium content of bones
Oximetry	Measurement of the oxygen content of blood
Paget's disease	Condition in which portions of bone are softened and enlarged
PEG tube	Percutaneous endoscopic gastrostomy-surgical placement of a feeding tube into the stomach
Permacath®	Vascular access catheters surgically inserted into a large vein for hemodialysis and plasmaphoresis
Phenytoin	An anticonvulsant medication
Plasmaphoresis	A procedure that separates the cellular portion of the blood from its liquid portion after which the cellular portion is cleansed and returned
Pons	Mid-portion of the brainstem that contains cranial nerve nuclei and major motor tracts
Pyridostigmine	A drug that blocks the breakdown of acetylcholine
QRS	Electrocardiographic waves representing the contraction of the main pumping chambers of the heart

REM	Rapid eye movement or dreaming sleep
Steroids	Potent anti-inflammatory medications
Succinylcholine	A rapidly acting neuro-muscular blocking agent used to paralyze skeletal muscle for surgical procedures
Tensilon®	Edrophonium-a rapidly acting drug that blocks the breakdown of acetylcholine, improving transmission of nerve impulses to muscle
Third nerve	The third cranial (oculomotor) nerve that controls eye movements and pupil size
Thrombolysis	Process of lysisng or dissolving blood clots
Thymus	A structure in the chest- part of the immune system
Tracheostomy	A surgical opening of the trachea for insertion of a tube necessary for protection of the airway
VA	Veterans Administration-a federal agency
Valproic acid	An anticonvulsant with uses in psychiatry
Vasospasm	Prolonged contraction of the smooth muscles of blood vessels, especially in the brain

Ventricle	A cavity containing fluid in the brain or the heart
V-fib	Ventricular fibrillation- a rapid and irregular contraction of the main pumping chamber of the heart, usually fatal
VRE	Vancomycin resistant enterococcus-another so-called super germ
Warfarin	Coumadin®-an oral anticoagulant